H. D. Lowry

**The happy Exile**

H. D. Lowry

**The happy Exile**

ISBN/EAN: 9783743346246

Manufactured in Europe, USA, Canada, Australia, Japa

Cover: Foto ©Andreas Hilbeck / pixelio.de

Manufactured and distributed by brebook publishing software (www.brebook.com)

H. D. Lowry

**The happy Exile**

THE·ARCADY·LIBRARY·
EDITED·BY·J·S·FLETCHER

THE·HAPPY
EXILE

# THE
# HAPPY EXILE

EDITED BY

## H. D. LOWRY

*WITH SIX ETCHINGS BY E. PHILIP PIMLOTT*

JOHN LANE, *The Bodley Head*
LONDON & NEW YORK
1898

Printed by BALLANTYNE, HANSON & Co.
At the Ballantyne Press

# EDITOR'S NOTE

*T*HE *papers here collected* are the work of one who
has *long forgotten the period of youthfulness they*
*chronicle.* Once *upon a time (let me explain to you)*
there **was** *a group of young men who worked hard for*
*little money, living gaily the while.* They made a play
*of their work,* **and the** *responsibilities that* **come with**
*settled incomes* **and positions of greater** or *less dignity,*
**had** *not yet fallen* **on** *them.*

*Now* **among all these there was none** *so utterly un-*
**bound as the man** *whose experiences* **you are to** *read.*
**He** *had a limitless affection for the society of the band,*
*and enjoyed* **the inexpensive dissipations** *that came in* the
*way of its members with a gusto never exceeded.* Yet
**he was** *one whose presence could never be counted upon,*
**unless a promise** *had been given ;* **and it** *was the habit*
*of his friends, at any meeting after a week during which*

# Editor's Note

they had not come across him, to inquire how he had
been faring in Cornwall.

For, indeed, he was no less truly a dweller beyond
the Tamar than in his London chambers near the sky.
There, as here, he had his friends. The interminable
journey he must take who would reach the real West
Country,

"*Where roses grow that have no thorns,*"

daunted him not at all. He was a veritable lover,
and would travel twenty dreary hours for the sake of
scarce as many in the land of his desire.

I found these papers awhile ago in a drawer where
he had bidden me search for an old article of his I
needed to consult. By his permission I carried them
away, and here you have them in print.

I had often wondered how he managed to content
himself down there in the country, nor had I found
much illumination in his frequent assurances that
there was "always plenty to do." These notes of
his experience gave me the explanation both of his
contentment and of his inability to account for it—
for he was the last man in the world to be altogether
reconciled to life as he found it.

He did nothing in the West, yet, as he had told me

# Editor's Note

so often, there was " always plenty to do." He stepped straightway into another world in leaving London, and found his own place in it awaiting him. He had his friends with whom to talk, and, if ever they were away from him, the come-and-go of the seasons and the slow progress of the Spring were enough to keep him occupied.

Concerning two of his papers I am a little in doubt. They can scarce have been written during the period when the open country began (so to speak) outside the door of his chambers. I can fancy they were produced after he had allowed himself to become a prisoner in London. The married man must have his occasional reflections, and he has surrendered many things in return for the privilege of owning his pretty house at Dulwich.

For the rest, these papers—chosen out of many—must speak for themselves. To me they have given pleasure as demonstrating that one man was at one time to be envied his happiness.

H. D. L.

Most of these Sketches and Studies have appeared in *The National Observer*, *Pall Mall Gazette*, *Black and White*, *The Speaker*, and *Chambers's*, by permission of whose Editors they are here reprinted

# CONTENTS

xiii

# Contents

# LIST OF ILLUSTRATIONS

# THE IDYL OF THE DAFFODILS

# THE IDYL OF THE
# DAFFODILS

" THROUGH happy, sunlit fields and quiet lanes,
  Where Spring had touched the branches into green,
  I wandered in the childhood of the year.
  For stormy March had come and raged his time,
  And now an April sunlight lit the land,
  And glistened in the drops of April rain,
  Or in the shallows of the brook.
                        Whenas
  The far off West grew splendid suddenly
  With sombre splendour of a dying sun,
  I laid me down in fields where lazy kine
  Browsed idly on the grass all green with Spring
  And bright with wide-strewn wealth of daffodils.
  Near me there went a little rain-fed stream
  That, from the distant hills to the far sea,
  Ran musically, ever murmuring.
  All things were peaceful as where, far away,
  Beneath a cloudless sky, in happy isles,
  The lotus-eater, wrapt in soft-hued dreams,
  Forgets the busy tumult of the world."

THAT is how the poem opens, and to the
end it is all in praise of Spring: a boyish
version of the tale of Echo and Narcissus,
owing its existence to the fact that a

schoolboy had been wont to wander in fields radiant "with all the golden pride of daffodils," and, wandering, had met with Love, companion of the Spring, who comes out of the West.

He was very young when he wrote it in his tiny study under the eaves, and if he could read it now—mine is the only surviving copy—he would undoubtedly perceive that what seemed to him a sure and certain warrant of future greatness was but his solitary piece of experience, naïvely set forth in blank verse differing from heroic couplets merely in the absence of rhymed endings.

Early in the poem, Echo meets the dreaming poet in a vale, which I fancy you would see if ever you should visit Torr's Steps, upon the Barle. At first she fancies him Narcissus, whom she is now to rejoin for a brief space as the reward of a long loneliness ; but soon she sees her error, and straightway the light of joy upon her countenance

> " Dies, as the sunlight dies upon the hills,
> When clouds are wafted from the windy sea."

Yet in a little while she takes courage, recognising him as a poet, since the land of their meeting is one whither poets and

their creatures alone may come ; and then
—as eagerly, it must be admitted, as though
she were a minor actress, and he the inter-
viewer of an illustrated weekly—she tells
him all her melancholy story, and of the
doom which angry Juno inflicted upon
her :

> " To live
> Eternally, a voice without a form :
> To wander through the ages o'er the world
> And still for evermore to be forbid
> To tell to kindly souls my deathless grief.
> Even as she spoke I faded from the form
> Of visible loveliness, and awhile I strayed
> Unresting o'er the earth.   I haunted woods
> And hollow glens on many a mountain-side ;
> For I might only mock the sounds I heard,
> Nor ever tell the grief that lived in me
> Save only when some lonely singer told
> The sorrows of his heart beneath the stars.
> Then softly did I sing them o'er again,
> And made them mine, and sang them o'er again,
> More softly and more sadly, till they died."

For that was the sort of memory he kept
of Jessie, though he had seen her face but
once without a smile upon it.

He had come to the school from a distance, and, perhaps because the accidents
of his upbringing had kept him unskilful in
the games they loved, his fellows, though
the best companions in the world, disconcerted him a little.   He was always glad

# The Idyl of the Daffodils

to be alone, and when the Spring had come
—or, indeed, as soon as the thrushes and
blackbirds had begun to make music for
an hour at dusk—it was his habit to cross
the road to a lane that led into the wide
fields, and yield himself to the enjoyment
of his dreams. There was no lack of occupation. A little stream came down from
the hills, and at every yard there was—or
there might be—a nest. Nor was the
delightfulness of this possibility one whit
diminished by the fact that he had never
known himself discover a nest unless he
trod on it: a thing which, being very
merciful, he never could have done inten-
tionally.

There was one place where the wanderer
could make sure of seeing a kingfisher if
he made the approach with sufficient quietness ; and sometimes there were fish leap-
ing up a diminutive cataract, where the
stream passed under an old grey bridge.
He had struck acquaintance with the
mistress of a certain farm-house ; her hos-
pitality most often took the form of cider
of a marvellous acerbity, and this the boy
detested so heartily he never failed to visit
her as he passed and taste it again. For
it seemed to him (so difficult did he find it
to swallow the draught without a grimace)

# The Idyl of the Daffodils

that if he refrained from visiting her, the honest matron must infallibly detect his reason for staying away.

But the thing that beyond all others drew him into the field was the fact that daffodils grew there as plentifully as daisies in other places, or kingcups by the river betwixt Bablockhithe and Godstow. The little stream runs between banks deep yet gently sloping, and here the pale gold of the flowers was rarer, though in this place it was wont to appear first. In the fields themselves you could pick a thousand yellow blooms without moving beyond a radius of some three or four yards. And this was ever the end of his wanderings, a bunch of daffodils the prize he took home.

Has it been said that he was afflicted with ridiculous shyness? There was a day when he came, happy in his mind, to the kissing-gate at the bottom of the lane. He had passed through the gateway, and retreat was no longer possible, when he looked ahead and for the first time set eyes upon Jessie. A huge elm tree had fallen from the earthen hedge across the lane, uprooted by a storm which had ushered in the moon of daffodils. The butt of it, cut off, lay in the ditch, the upper part stretched from the

# The Idyl of the Daffodils

hedge-top into the next field, and a girl was sitting on it, idle and self-possessed, her pretty feet dangling.

There was no escaping the ordeal. The boy advanced with timid fears, and vainly strove to pass the girl. But she would not let him alone.

"Give me a daffodil, pretty boy," she said.

Now the boy was not pretty, but he was very much a boy. Without regarding her he chose a flower from the bunch and held it towards her.

" I can't reach," she said, plaintively.

He looked up. She was laughing in the depths of her grey eyes ; her lips were parted ; the hair was all in ringlets round her pretty head. And the boy forgot his fears.

" Take them all," he said, holding up the bunch.

" But don't you want them ?" she said. She had taken the bunch and was arranging it with dainty touches, never looking at him.

The boy flushed hotly.

" May I have one of them back ? I want that."

Then she looked at him again, and her smile flashed out.

8

# The Idyl of the Daffodils

" Good boy," she said, encouragingly.

She was a long time in choosing the flower he had asked, but presently she bent down, holding it between her fingers. The boy took it, hardly knowing what to do with it, and greatly disconcerted by the laughing eyes bent upon him. But still he could not go.

" What is your name ? " he asked, trembling at his own audacity.

" They call me Jessie," said the girl.

" I have never seen you before," he said, as if he strove to excuse an ignorance beyond pardon.

" And yet I come this way very often when I have a holiday," she answered, with a touch of his own shyness.

The boy left her presently, with a vague impression that her time was spent mostly in some wonderful region lying outside the limits of this dull earth. It was not till later he learned that, dainty as she was in all things, she was only a little milliner. There were words she could not speak quite correctly, and the knowledge of them was a treasure to the boy : he had a poetry all to himself.

All that day, and for a long time after, he kept a watch upon the masters, and upon elder boys whom he had hitherto

respected hugely, wondering if they were
his brothers or his inferiors : if they possessed, or had been denied, the dear experience that was making life so good to
him.    And the wonder grew as the Spring
waxed greener, and he had more and more
knowledge of the mysteries which had
dawned on him when Jessie besought him
for a daffodil.

I would give much to have had him
under observation at this time ; for they
met frequently, and he must have grown
wonderfully in the few weeks this idyl was
in progress.

There is no such moment in a man's
life ('tis said), as that wherein some worshipped one of the other sex first recognises
his devotion by using him as a possession
of her own.    And the boy has told me of
an occasion when he was suffering from a
cold of some severity, and the path which
led them across a ploughed field was so
narrow that only one could walk on it.
Jessie insisted that he should occupy it,
and he (of course) upon his right of self-
sacrifice for her sake.    But she would not
hear of his disobeying the dictates of herself and Prudence (reconciled for once !)
and in the end the boy submitted and took
the path, while Jessie walked on the red

earth at his side. Now and again he coughed laboriously. A king might have envied him.

The idyl reached its end at last, when the boy had to leave for his holidays in a far and desolate country where Jessie was not. They parted under a flowering chestnut by the little bridge, on whose grey stones were carved the names of a hundred lovers who had been happy where these twain were miserable.

" You will not forget me ? " she said.

" How could I ? " asked the boy, indignantly : for he was at the blessed age when in parting one has at least the relief of believing one's regret will be eternal.

" There will be others," hinted Jessie.

" There is none like you," he declared indignantly. " But there will be others for you. It is I who may be forgotten."

Jessie looked at him, her big eyes grave for once, and thrice lovelier so than in the mirth which had first dazzled him. But laughter came into them very quickly ; for she also believed that these things last.

" Foolish ! " she cried. " How should I forget ? Good-bye."

The boy left her under the chestnut, and on the morrow went into that far and desolate country where she was not. Spring was there also, and country children, coming in to the Board School, brought bunches of primroses every morning as a gift for their favourite teachers. But to the boy it was a barren Spring; and girls, whom he had hitherto been able to disregard, worried and troubled him for the one reason that they were not Jessie.

A little poem, that some one has since translated out of a foreign tongue, may be taken as the expression of his emotions at this period.

"Once I said, There is none like her; no woman is beautiful but she. I was glad they could not see how you were lovely.

"But now. . . . . Why do they mock me so, the women who are not beautiful? There is not one but has something that was once yours only; often I hear your laughter in the street. Every moment I see you, and every moment say, It is not she.

"For you are yonder where the sea is, and I may not come to you. . . . . Why does the wind blow always out of the west?"

The days drew on until the time of his banishment from Elysian fields was ended. But the Spring was dead, and with it Jessie had passed out of his life. Whether she indeed died (as he then believed), or merely went into another region to dwell, he never surely discovered. But she never came again to the fields where he had

# The Idyl of the Daffodils

found her, and so in time she dwelt in his memory as a lonely, sad-eyed creature, wandering forlorn "along the mead of asphodel" and seeking—whom but himself? Whence, a little while later, arose the poem to which I have ventured this reference, and whereof if he remembered its existence amid the more serious affairs that now engross him, the boy would doubtless be most heartily ashamed.

# THE NEW CONTENTMENT

# THE NEW CONTENTMENT

SOMEHOW it has not been granted me to know the loveliness of this dear country until to-day, when I take my farewell. Day after day went by and left the longings February wakened unappeased by any realisation of the Spring. I was like one who has been so long an exile that he forgets his mother tongue, and in his own home finds himself a stranger. But now that I must go it seems an impious thing to quit the fields and seek the city. Spring is come, and though my vague desires are all unsatisfied, I rejoice to-day in a new contentment.

The night was one of frequent showers, coming opportunely to break up a long drought; the morning sky was softly grey. Even at noon there was no brightening; but now the pale blue sky is radiant with sunshine and the long low clouds shine dazzlingly. Everywhere the giant gorse is golden with close-packed bloom. Looking south, you can scarcely tolerate the

# The New Contentment

blaze of it; towards the colder north it seems to be little more than a constituent in the colouring of its dull and wind-worn spikes. But, in the one way or the other, you perceive it everywhere: it fills barren crofts, and beautifies the ugly waste-heaps of abandoned mines. Look where you will, no hedge can be descried that is not thus gloriously crowned.

And it is well to let the eyes go far afield, for every dint of the horizon shows a glimpse of the blue sea. It must be hot now on the small white beaches, and because I must needs go from their neighbourhood to-morrow I am assured that many days like this will come: days when it would suffice for occupation to lie in the sun and watch great waves of palest chrysoprase rise, then curl to break, while the white of the foamy summits flickers on the clear inner curve, and the blithe wind blows a smoke of brine along the advancing line.

The fields are green at last, save where the late-sown wheat is hardly risen, Here the rooks are abroad in shining raiment, and the magpies are beyond the eager counting of the superstitious. You may see them in companies of six and eight, flying wide and high like pigeons, and fighting in the air. The larks are singing, and of all the birds that haunt the gorse patches the gayest is the yellow-hammer. Everywhere the silver of the blackthorn (though fallen from its first plentitude) accompanies the gold of the gorse.

Most beautiful of all, though leafless yet, are graceful palm shrubs which stand in the waste places. They are gloriously arrayed in catkins, that appear as centres of misty radiance as you catch them against the sun. The same radiance is taken by the bunchy green leaves of the hawthorns.

The daffodils are already almost over; but, indeed, the daffodil is at all times rather the herald of the Spring than a proper member of her gay companionship. And at least there is no place left bare by the dog-violets, no hedge or coppice where you cannot gather primroses by handfuls. Damned in London, one will dream deliciously of the coolness of their petals held against the face on moist Spring mornings.

The woods that line the valleys are good to look on. In one the small oaks are still untouched of the new life; only dead leaves and withered bracken are visible, and the dull silver of trunks and branches. In one a haze of purple hovers, as it were, above the contour of the wood, and the buds are manifestly bursting.

# The New Contentment

Wood-pigeons croon in the heart of it, having their nest in a sycamore, whose golden-brown foliage, as it was first to come, shall be the first to wither and fall in autumn. They have built there every year since one who has felt himself very aged upon occasions was a young child. They must be very old now!

But the loveliest wood of all lies upon the slope of a hillside, beyond a marsh whose sword-grass tussocks almost dam the stream they hide. Tall pine-trees mount to the hill's summit; below, above the stream, are tasselled larches enveloped in a tender emerald mist. Primroses shine like stars from among the tiny beeches (still laden with dead leaves) that grow beneath. One place has wood-sorrel in the shadow of its granite boulders; another is beautiful with frail anemones; now and again you catch the sound of falling water, and the birds make (as one might say) an atmosphere of song.

Of a truth, it is foolish to seek the city. All deeds are contemptible and unworthy the doing while there is the chance of idleness here. But holidays must end; and I might have lost the beauty of to-day had I not come forth conscious of the change appointed.

# A SCANDAL IN ARCADY

THE smallest incident is so much talked of here in Arcady that one comes to comprehend it far more thoroughly than townfolk understand the details of a sensational case, a suburban "horror," a Cabinet crisis. A really important event quickly becomes as it were, a part of the personal experience of every man who dwells in the region where it happened ; and so there is no one in all the country round about Trelorne who could not write the history that follows, though the events are of no later date than last Sunday's.

Spring had come, after a long season of frost ; but Emanuel Kemp and his wife had had little chance of noticing the blessed change, inasmuch as they were both engaged in teaching at a Board School some two miles distant from the village. They had but scant opportunities to live their lives ; to enjoy life for its own sake, and realise the goodness of the world. Thyrza had her household duties to attend to when she got release from school duties. 'Manuel was a local preacher, and his sermons were in such request that a great part of his leisure was given to their preparation and delivery. He was something of a musician, too and on those Sundays when he happened to have no "appointment" he sang in the choir at the little chapel, adding a lusty baritone to Thyrza's pretty treble.

They had been married but two years, and they loved one another almost foolishly. Yet there were some who felt—though they would never have dared to express it— a certain pity for Thyrza, in that she was wedded to a man so very serious as her husband. I had my doubts of their wisdom, but shared in their error, having once witnessed, myself unseen, a lovely outbreak of mad youthfulness in this pretty Board-schoolmistress.

Last Sunday was the most exquisite day of the year: the one of all others that will dwell in memory as having been the occasion of Spring's final triumph. It was not long after six when 'Manuel arose and, having lit the fire and prepared himself a cup of tea, made his way down the coombe towards the chapel, there to attend a " class-meeting." The larks were singing

one against the other in magnificent rivalry;
the gorse flamed golden ; and every way-
side bush gave protection to a blackbird
that fled shrieking as the schoolmaster
drew near. In one place the road began to
climb the hillside obliquely, and he looked
down to the sea. Then the ascent became
more direct. He mounted, descended again
into another valley, and in a few minutes
had reached the chapel.

The class in which he "met" consisted
of no more than half a dozen aged men.
All had been miners in youth and manhood,
and therefore their decrepitude was greater
than their years appeared to warrant. They
sang the chosen hymns so quaveringly that
'Manuel was half-ashamed of the strength
and clearness of his own voice, and only
felt at his ease when the meeting was far
advanced. But when it came to praying
everything was changed : the old men
began, each in his turn, with voices almost
inaudible, hesitating greatly ; but a rapture
took each presently, and he prayed with a
vigorous passion that left him utterly exhausted, even as those who prophesy are
exhausted and worn out when they have
spoken. They came out into the sunlight
with something of the rapture still upon
their faces.

# A Scandal in Arcady

'Manuel walked a little way with one of the elder men ; but he was glad when they had come to the parting of the ways, for he was conscious that his enjoyment of the morning almost went beyond the bounds of decorum.   This same enjoyment of the world was the cause of some slight conflict within him as he went homeward ; he wanted to get back to Thyrza, and at the same time was conscious that on such a day to hurry over anything would be to commit the sin of ingratitude to Providence.   Yet he went more and more quickly at every step, and in the end he was glad he had made haste.   Thyrza stood waiting for him at the gate of their little garden, and blew a kiss to him while he was still afar off. He returned the greeting at the gate, regardless of appearances ; and she held up a little bunch of dewy violets for him to smell.

"Aren't they sweet?" she asked, delightedly.   "But come in quickly.   Breakfast is ready, and I haven't long to spare.

The schoolmaster took off his good black coat and hung it carefully behind the door, while Thyrza filled the teapot with boiling water.   By the time the tea was ready everything else was on the table ; and they took their seats on opposite sides. the sunlight streaming in upon them through the flowers and leaves of Thyrza's window-plants.

"Have you been out at all?" asked 'Manuel. "Have you seen and felt what fashion morning it is?"

"I felt it while I slept, I think," she said, adding the milk to his tea. Then, looking at him across the table with an expression that seemed above all things to testify of her youthfulness, she added, "'Tis a day to make holiday. Teaching—I can't bear the thought of it to-day, for to-day I'm all too young. But there's the Sunday-school as soon as we've done breakfast."

'Manuel hesitated a little while. When he spoke it was in a diction singularly correct, and without the slight trace of the dear local cadence he usually allowed himself in private life. "I don't see that you need to go this morning," he said. "After all, the first duty of man and wife is to be man and wife. 'Tis little enough I see of you. Let the school take care of itself for to-day. We'll sit in the garden.

Thyrza laughed at him across the table, a very child again. "Is it you that's speaking?" she cried. "I can hardly believe it."

"Perhaps not," her husband answered.

" But 'twould be foolishness to go to school to-day. I can't fancy the Lord meant days like this to go unenjoyed."

"Well," said Thyrza, "we'll enjoy it. But there's chapel in an hour." She ended with a sigh, and, strangely enough, it was echoed in her husband's answer.

"Yes!" he said. "I suppose we can't neglect that. But, at any rate, we have an hour."

They went into the garden, 'Manuel still in his shirt-sleeves. There was little enough to see. The frost was not long over, and it had lasted until the villagers, accustomed to a climate temperate alike in summer and in winter, had begun to fancy all germs of life must be killed, and the earth destined to barrenness until it should have been revivified by sunlight and the warm breath of the West. Yet there were signs of the new life; and on this morning the slightest tokens were things to notice. 'Manuel was commonly supposed to be a person of great sobriety; but men often love their opposites, and Thyrza laughed and babbled to-day as she had done when they were lovers.

The hour passed very swiftly; but the schoolmaster took no note of its going. Thyrza was more observant. " Do you know 'tis nearly chapel-time ? " she asked. " I suppose we must be getting ready." She looked at him, laughing, and her eyes asked shamelessly what she would never have dared to put into words.

'Manuel examined his big silver watch, regarding it with an air of suspicion which no previous irregularities in its working had justified. " I suppose we must," he said, unwillingly. " But——"

"'Tis a lovely morning," said Thyrza, stooping to brush a fragment of dry grass from the skirt of her dress. She would have gone to school, had not her husband intervened ; but one taste of liberty had made her long for more.

The schoolmaster hesitated for a little. Then he spoke with an air of desperate resolve. "We won't go to chapel," he said. " We'll go out and look at the world to-day. Run in and find a hat."

He ended with immense solemnity ; and even Thyrza, when she returned, had the look of a pretty child who ventures upon some unparalleled rebellion against authority. Nor can you wonder.

For night had not fallen when all the world knew of what these two had done that morning : of their deserting chapel and Sunday-school alike. And it was not a mere desertion. After the service was over certain serious people were going homeward through a lane not far from the schoolmaster's house. Their grave conversation was suddenly disturbed by the sound of laughing voices, and, while they still wondered, they turned a corner and beheld a spectacle whereof every man of us seems in his own thought to have been a witness.

Thyrza, with a biggish bunch of primroses and dusty catkins in her hand, was standing in the lane, looking up to where the schoolmaster stood upon the top of the hedge. His respectable black clothes were muddy and in the wildest disarray. He was struggling in a tangle of brambles and thorns, while he endeavoured to secure the scattered daffodils to which Thyrza was directing him. He did not observe the approach of the new-comers; but Thyrza's voice was suddenly hushed, and at last, missing its music, he turned and saw them. His jaw dropped, and as the procession advanced, it was once or twice evident that he desired and was striving to say something. But the power of speech had utterly deserted him, and the horrified spectators of his madness passed without a word.

Since then he has manifestly lived under

# A Scandal in Arcady

the shadow of a trouble that never lets itself be forgotten ; and, indeed, he is like to suffer for his imprudence in more ways than one. It can hardly be argued by his strongest friend that such a man is fitted to discharge the duties either of school-master or of local preacher. But I met Thyrza in the village yesterday, and for the first time knew for certain that we, who had thought her choice a mistake, had shown ourselves no less foolish than the mass of busybodies.

"A lovely morning !" I said.

"Yes !" she answered, with the gayest smile. "The Spring is come at last."

# THE WEDDING MORNING

# THE WEDDING MORNING

Frost in these temperate regions by the sea is a thing for the sight of which men polish their spectacles and go forth wondering. But lately it came and abode with us, staying so long that the oldest inhabitant was at last compelled to admit that he remembered no such rigorous season. Usually we have daffodils and narcissi, to say nothing of pale primroses, in February. Last year the camellias that grow in the open against the northern wall of a certain old-time garden, were all but over before that month was ended, and the rhododendrons were in the full glory of their bloom. This year it had been otherwise. The camellias were melancholy spectacles of blighted buds ; acres of wallflowers were indubitably ruined ; and the broccoli, by whose culture we get the chief part of our living, were in such a condition that even Londoners

35

could hardly be expected to find them palatable.

It does not take many days of frost to do damage to the extent of several thousands of pounds in the region lying round about our village, and long before the frost was over the market-gardeners were dolorously declaring themselves on the verge of bankruptcy. Upon reflection one must admit that they said the same thing last year. We believed them then; but this year we had the fields themselves for evidence that they spoke truthfully.

It seemed the frost would never end; yet those who knew the country and loved it well could not believe this hardness of the crust went deeper. Underneath that iron-grey face, they fancied the good earth was still warm and soft and fertile, and the seeds in it swelling and ready to send up green leaves and flowers at the first opportunity. "If there was a bit of a soft to come by night," we said to one another every morning as we looked upon the frozen fields, and shivered in the unaccustomed cold, "'twould be all right again in a few hours."

Our faith was justified by the event. One night those who had been sleepless because of the cold realised suddenly that

# The Wedding Morning

they had no desire to sleep, being so happy
all at once, and so reconciled to life. And
while they lay awake and wondered what
had befallen, there came a sound of the
wind rising and after it the noise of rain
at the window. The wind had gone into
the west, and the reign of the frost was
ended. The fall of the Chaldean who
reigned in Babylon came not more suddenly ; and the knowledge of the change
had somehow reached the sleeping while
they dreamt, so that they had it when they
woke.

Of late one's bed had grown warm only
in the morning, long after the miserable
dawn had come. We had all been sluga-
beds and unashamed, since none of us was
worse than his neighbour. But on this
morning one might have fancied he had
played the Rip Van Winkle for a month
at least, and that in a single night the
proper hour of rising had grown earlier
in the same degree. For the sun was
shining, and huge dazzling clouds swept
inland over the pale blue sky. The bay
(which had been leaden-hued and melan
choly and land-locked for a month or
more) was filled with white-caps, and
the noise of the sea was in the air. The
birds were singing, perched in the top

# The Wedding Morning

branches of leafless trees now visibly budding, and every sparrow had a feather in its beak.

So we rose early and went out into gardens or into the street (where the pleasure of the change was trebled by the fact that we could talk of it with others); and when a certain father of ten announced that he "felt like a boy again," there was a chorus of " So do I." It was the maddest of mornings. People who had been dying the day before stood at their doorways, or, at least, sat in the sunlight in their gardens; and if you made inquiries as to their health they answered in tones that made you wonder again if you had not been sleeping for a month or more: for you seemed to remind them by your questioning of a thing so long past as to be hardly worth remembering.

Strangely enough—for things do not usually happen at the right moment in our imperfectly ordered life—there was a wedding at the little chapel that stands at the head of the street. The village, it should be said, is one long street, lying betwixt low hills and the sea, and the bride had to drive along the whole length of it on her way to the chapel. Everything went right that morning: she was

# The Wedding Morning

pretty, as all girls should be on the first day of Spring, and those who knew her swore that in her case beauty had worked outwards from the centre of her being. "Good as gold, she is," I heard said by half a hundred; but it is more than possible that the most notorious shrew would have had a quite triumphal progress through the village had she chosen to get married on this day, when marrying seemed the one thing in the world worth doing. I saw her pass towards the chapel, the people flocking after her to get a sight of the ceremony. There was not one of them but had a store of rice, and many a dress bulged with hidden slippers.

"'Tis the fate of us all, sooner or later," I said. "Upon my soul, I envy the happy bridegroom."

Samuel, my companion, sighed. "I've been through it," he said, "but somehow I do wish to-day one could start again at the beginning. 'Tis a day to make a married man wonder what place there is for him to fill in the world. But your duty is plain."

I laughed. "Come over to the Mount," I said. "By your own showing we have no business here."

So we turned from the neighbourhood of

# The Wedding Morning

the chapel, and went down the granite steps to the beach. The waves were breaking splendidly, the white of their wild crests shining and disappearing in the inner curve like summer lightning. The stone causeway to the Mount had only just emerged. We crossed, and made the circuit of that "hoar rock in the sea," speaking but little because the wind beat in freshly from the wide sea and made conversation troublesome. Moreover, there were things to note so numerous that we forgot the natural desire of friends to talk with one another.

It may have been the magic influence of that one night of rain and the west wind; or perhaps the spectacle was new only because we had not ventured thus far from home while the frost was upon us. At any rate, the wonderful narcissi were all in flower, star-like among their green spears; and there were tiny daffodils, more lovely in their untouched simplicity than the double things that grew near them. A score of small birds rose as we advanced and flew onward to another rock, where they perched and posed until we were close at hand again, when they went onward just a little farther. An otter was fishing a hundred yards out, lying on his side upon the water, as each

# The Wedding Morning

successive wave came in, and letting it pass under him. Once or twice he dived, and when at last he came to the surface with a small male pollack in his mouth, we could have cheered at his success, though the most callous man might have pitied even a fish whose doom it was to die on such a day. The otter came in, swimming hand-over-hand, as it were, and we saw him vanish under a pile of boulders. We passed onward, pausing a long while to watch the antics of a peacock in the sun-shine. Lastly, we set forth again along the causeway to the mainland. We had a full view of the village and the hills beyond, and they had somehow put on a new loveliness.

"I never knew," said Samuel, "I never knew before that Jacka's plantation looked so good as that." We mounted the granite steps just in time to see the pretty bride go off a happy wife. We watched the trap recede, and when at last it disappeared Samuel turned to me with a face inimitably solemn.

"It is not good for man to live alone. My son, 'tis time that you were married." A lark sprang into the clear air from the hillside beyond the houses, and sang rapturously.

# The Wedding Morning

I looked laughingly at my friend. "Well," I said, "you have but to find a bride. Only . . . . I ask nothing selfishly; but, for the day's sake, do you see to it that she is beautiful."

# A ROMANTIC CONFESSION

# A ROMANTIC CONFESSION

I HAD come down through the night, and now, issuing into the streets of Tallywarn, could hardly realise that I had ever been away. As of old, the rain dripped steadily out of a forlorn grey sky ; the roadway was but an archipelago of standing pools, the streets well-nigh deserted. An aged gentlemen stood beneath the granite portico of the Literary Institution, his umbrella held half open as he gazed irresolutely at the hurrying passers-by. Finally, I came to the barber's shop, and beheld William Trethewy, its proprietor, gazing disconsolately over the whitened lower panes of his window. I had no definite purpose set before me ; the sight convinced me I could not do better than enter and talk with him. He started forward with a sudden briskness as I entered and hung my hat upon a peg, welcoming me to the town with not a little *empressement*. I took a seat and bade him cut my hair.

# A Romantic Confession

Then I sat silent, while he discoursed of the recent history of Tallywarn.

William Trethewy is now proprietor of the shop, but there was a time when he was only a servant. Indeed, his earliest connection with the establishment was in the capacity of lather-boy on Saturdays, and he had served thus for a year or two before he rose to the dignity of regular assistant. And at the age of twenty-two, when he had become a person of some importance in virtue of his acquaintance with the unwritten history of the district, he had astonished the people of Tallywarn by quitting the post and going up to London to improve himself. Seeing that he was already the most admired of all who practised his craft for miles around, the step he had taken was deemed a ridiculous superfluity. But when he returned for a holiday, two years later, he spent some part of the time in the shop of his late employer, and for pure kindness showed certain of the best customers how up-the-country barbers did their work. The master reaped a splendid harvest of pennies (for the charge only rose to three-halfpence if you refused to sponge your own face, and had a touch of the powder-puff), but ever afterwards he suffered in reputation. For

# A Romantic Confession

weeks after William Trethewy's shaving
was a common topic of conversation; and
when he returned, a year later, to become
the partner of his late employer, he immediately took rank as the important man of
the two. Old Mr. Tregaskis retired more
and more into the background; finally he
became in effect a sleeping partner, only
emerging into publicity on Saturday, when
there was work for two. On the day of
my return to Tallywarn he had been dead
so long that the younger patrons of the
shop used to ask why it was invariably
referred to as "Tregaskis's," albeit owned
by Trethewy.

We had talked of many things. Then,
as I sat with eyes closed while he cut the
hair upon my forehead, "Well," he said,
"I suppose you're glad to be back again,
sir?"

"Why, yes," I answered. "Even this
wretched weather seems no more than
natural—a sort of welcome—now that one
is back in Tallywarn."

"'Tis lonely in London?" he continued.

"Sometimes," I answered.

"Yes," he said, "I was fine an' lonely
sometimes, when I was up there. There
was a mad fancy come into my head one
day when I was like that: I was young,

and you can never tell what a young man 'll think upon next. Moreover, with a young man to think upon a thing is to do it."

He paused and snipped with absurd delicacy at imaginary hairs. "Is it a story?" I asked.

"Well," he said, speaking with an evident relief, "there's only one person do know it beside myself, and she didn't know it until after she was my wife. But I can fancy you might understand.

"I was up there two years to begin with, and lived hard, being resolved to come back to this shop with money to do things never dreamt of before in Tallywarn. Some are done this long time; some must wait their turn. Well, after two years I took a holiday, and I wadn' home a day before all my plans were changed. George Restarick lived next door to father, and he had a niece stopping with him—Janie Restarick, from Trewavas. She was a little bit of a thing, and I shouldn' go beyond pity with a man that couldn' see her good looks. But she had more than looks : it was like all the maids that ever you met, schemin' and charmin' in one little body. No man could stand against her. Now he would think he could have

# A Romantic Confession

her for the asking, and only keep silence because **the thing** was all too good for belief; **and the** next moment he would know (certainly, as a man **sick** and sleepless do **know that** he must die) **that** he **was** nothing in the **world** to her, and never would be. And somehow when he was most hopeless, and swearing **never to go** near her again, he would be most carried away to do **foolish** things **for her** pleasure. 'Twas that **way** with **me for the** fortnight of my holiday, and I left her still in Tally-warn, **when I had to go** back. After that I didn' lack **for** company. There was such a crowd of hopes, fears, plottings, and plan-nings : 'twas continual bewilderment.

"Now, one Friday night in the month of June, I came forth from the shop very late. **I was tired out,** and more than a bit downhearted; **but all at once the wind** came against **my face,** soft **and cool as** sleep itself, and I didn' **need to look at the sky** to note that **the wind** was **from the** west. The wind went by, **and then I** could almost fancy I heard the noise of the **sea** behind it, and the tears came **into my eyes.** And there, up against the wall, was a great **bill in** red and white, telling of cheap **trains to** Cornwall the next day, being **the Saturday** before Whit-Monday.

# A Romantic Confession

My mind was made up as I read, and I couldn' think I had ever been tired. I got home quickly, and the next morning took a little handbag to the shop. Master was a great one for getting all the fresh air he could, and would spend all his time, from Saturday closing time to nine o'clock on Monday packed in a train with other fools, so that none should ever say of him that he didn' make the best use of his leisure. So when I asked if I could leave early that night, because I was thinking to go a long journey, he didn' need pressing.

" At eleven o'clock I left the place. I was on the Underground for something under a lifetime, and a little after midnight the train slipped out of Paddington, making towards Tallywarn and Trewavas. I was awake all the night, though often enough I kept my eyes closed, being wishful to think my own thoughts.

" I told 'ee what fashion maid she was. Whenever the train stopped, I was daggin' for it to get forward ; and as soon as ever we had started again, the wheels as they went round would be saying, plain as speaking, ' You *fool*, you *fool*, you *fool*, you *fool*,' and Janie's face would look at me out of the darkness, laughing at me.

" Seeming to me, we stopped everywhere.   It was chapel time when we came to Tallywarn.   I sat back and kept out of sight, for it seemed a sinful thing to pass by like a stranger and not stay to see my own people.   But in a moment we were moving again, and then there was no more thinking possible until I had left the train and started to walk out to Trewavas.   I suppose 'tis a trifle over five miles if you go by the cliffs.   The sun was shining, and overhead more larks than a man could keep count of; and the noise of the sea was like a voice whispering all the time that I was home again.   I knew Janie would be in chapel now, and so I sat down against a little sandy hill.

"Then all the trouble began again.   I could see it plain as daylight: I was a fool to have come down, wasting time and money, and running the risk of vexing my own people, for the sake of being a few miles nearer to a little maid that cared no more for me than for half a hundred others that happened to be in love with her.   I wished myself back in London; I wished I had never set eyes upon her; once I said aloud, 'I wish she was dead,' and afterwards sat in fear for full ten minutes, knowing that the maddest prayers are oftenest answered.   And then sleep came upon me slowly and yet suddenly at the last, and I forgot the bother of my thoughts. I can mind that just before I went off, I spoke her name once or twice, very softly, and tacking on to it all the foolish words I might have called her by if she had cared at all and been there beside me.

" I was tired out and lay all day in the sun, almost waking once or twice, then sleeping again when I heard the sound of the sea, as a child 'll sleep when the mother sings softly. But at last I woke shivering, and found I had slept until chapel-time was come round again. So I walked quickly towards Trewavas, and when I had come to the higher part of the town I turned in at a little inn and had some food. When I came out they were just coming from church and chapel, and the road above the bay was full of young men and maidens laughing and love-making as they strolled up and down. I went through the winding little streets to the place where Janie Restarick lived : I stood and waited.

" There was a light inside and the harmonium was playing. I could hear her voice, that I should know though all the angels in Heaven stood singing with her. And again I was certain she was not for me. I stood there, maybe, for more than

# A Romantic Confession

an hour. Then the singing ceased; the door opened, a young man stepped forth, and I saw Janie standing in the doorway. Then, as she went in again, I knew that it was hopeless. I turned away and went back to the inn. In the morning, just as all the world was waking, ready for Whitsun games, I turned my back upon Trewavas and took train for London.

" I was on the road all day, and all day long I could see Janie, in her pretty new frock, dancing in the rings with a crowd of chaps, or walking in the procession, the brass band leading, and hundreds looking on. I was near maddened with thoughts that wouldn' let me rest. Now I was certain I had done well to come back, but mad to think I had gone down ; and then again I could feel the kiss she would have given me if I had gone forth and spoken when I saw her at the door. And when I came to Paddington, and went on a 'bus through the noisy streets, I could swear she was just going off alone with the young man I saw leave the house, the moonlight on them, and both glad to be quiet together after so many noisy games. And that thought gave me wisdom ; being so certain I had nothing to lose, I should have been a fool not to try whether there might be anything to gain. I reached my lodgings, and sat down at once to write a letter.

" 'Dear Maid,' I said, 'will 'ee promise to marry me when I do come back to Tallywarn? I've been longin' for 'ee ever since I was home last, and get no rest for thinkin' of 'ee.' "

Trethewy had still made pretence to be trimming my hair while he told his story. Now he was silent and bent himself assiduously to his task.

"Well?" I said.

"Why, all my fears was foolishness!" he said. "She wrote a word or two by the next post, and it seems the maid had lost her heart when first I give her mine. Now was I a fool or not? Have 'ee ever felt like such a thing yourself?"

He took the towel from around my neck and stood back, regarding me. I laughed as I arose, but made no directer answer. For I conceive that no man is compelled to bear witness against himself —least of all, by a confession of his un-committed follies.

# ON SUNDAY MORNING

# ON SUNDAY MORNING

IT was a sultry night at best. I was vaguely certain that none slept soundly throughout the house. For myself, I quickly abandoned hope and patience. Two o'clock struck and found me wide awake ; it wanted a few minutes to three when I rose and thrust aside the blind, gazing out into the empty square.

I think it is Hawthorne has noted that the summer day in England is a thing without beginning and without end : always, when you arise the sunny world seems to have been a long time waiting for you ; always, when night has fallen, you may discern some foreshadowings of the day to come. This is doubtless true enough ; yet I dare fancy I arose at the very initial moment of the day.

Even as I looked from my window the sparrows began to twitter ; clouds of dull purple, huge and very low-built, passed and disappeared before a breeze from the north-west, like giant creatures—remote in all their attributes alike from brute and human denizens of the day—homing after the night's harmless revelries. A cock crowed heavily, and as I stepped into the street a thrush awoke and sang in some neighbouring garden. A moment later it was plain there were full a dozen inhabiting by-places of the town; and I was no sooner come to the fields (where the town ends abruptly, with no inter-space of gardened suburbs), than I paused with a feeling of amazement at the multiplicity of noises that fulfilled the new day.

There were thrushes and blackbirds without number; cocks were crowing far and near, and from a rookery hard by came the noise of a large colony of rooks, awake and preparing for activity. A cuckoo sounded his baffling note; and somewhere a gull was crying in the dusk: so that one might almost have expected to come upon a strange man, supernaturally old, seeking cover with some nefarious burden borne upon a rusty wheelbarrow. The sounds increased in variety as I kept on towards the sea: never a bush but some small bird was vastly angered that one should come near his seat. The rooks appeared, solemnly faring forth into the fields. A couple of hares, playing in a huge ploughed field, had the appearance of animals greatly bigger : they might have been greyhounds.

Some two miles beyond the town the ground in front of one slopes up steeply to the cliffs ; the valley one has been following hitherto is merged in that which lies at the foot of the slope, running at right angles to the path from the town. The foot of the descent is wooded, and upon the outskirts of the copse were rabbits without number. Chancing to look over a gate I beheld a youngster of a few weeks standing but half a dozen yards from me. I kept still ; the rabbit, sitting on his haunches, with ears erect and motionless, looked very steadily at the hedge before him, with not even a side glance at the gate where I was leaning. I waited, mildly interested, thinking he would go ; but still he held himself motionless—sphinx-like, almost—and manifested a stern resolve to outstay me. I had a certain curiosity to see how he would comport himself, but presently the situation became embarrassing ; I moved, ever so slightly, and in an instant the rabbit was gone.

Your rabbit, I take it, is at all ages a very ridiculous creature, calling loudly for good-tempered caricature. Consider the alarm of the full-grown animal on your approach : is it not vastly suggestive of a buxom, well-attired spinster who gathers her skirts about her and braves the confusion of cabs and omnibuses in some meeting-place of busy thoroughfares? And the bumpy, jumpy youngster : what is he but the great " switch-back " idea absurdly translated into flesh and blood? I have assuredly as little as most men of the national ardour for slaughter, but a certain comicality inherent in the sport makes rabbit-shooting simply irresistible.

The Wild Birds Protection Act is an invention of these latter days ; yet I can scarce believe we are more humane than those that were before us. In the old days, no man set fire to the heather after the end of March, when birds are nesting ; the modern savage takes a particular delight in firing the waste when its rusty brown is just upon the point of glorification with a glow of purple bloom. On this Sunday morning I found a great tract desolate and black, and, seeing it, moved forward with anger at my heart. And then (do you remember the Autocrat's quotation from the *Houyhnhums' Gazette?*) I was crossing the blackened space by a narrow track,

# On Sunday Morning

whose turf had been too worn to suffer by the fire ; the scent of the burnt peat was in my nostrils, and under that magical influence my emotions suffered an immediate change.

It is curious, by-the-bye, that though ferns, brambles, and thistles are scarcely to be noticed amid the growing heather, they are always the first to show signs of life after the fire has passed over them. In certain places which were burnt last year the heather had not apparently begun to grow again ; but every charred stem of the gorse was ringed about at the earth's surface with young shoots ; and the warm brown of the earth, set with young brambles glistening ferns, and the milky thistles dear to rabbits in captivity, had an exquisite beauty of colouring as one looked over it towards the sun.

Somehow the seaward aspect failed to please. The faces of the cliffs were still unvisited of the sun ; a sort of gloomy twilight hung about them, and to look down upon the tiny desolate beaches was to learn that it was still early in the morning—to be well-nigh convinced of folly, in that one was afield thus early. Towards the east the waters shone like steel ; upon the other hand they were incarnadined with ruddy water from the tin-mines, which enters the

sea beyond the furthest visible headland,
and had been brought around it by the
westerly wind. But all this was a matter
of the very smallest import: the narrow
tract of waste land afforded a sufficient occupation and interest.

And thus in idleness the time passed
quickly: very soon I was aware of growing
hunger, and turned to go back the way I
had come. Down in the valley, where it
looks upon the woods, a cuckoo was singing
with an energy that compelled particular
attention. I wondered for a moment at
his remarkable persistency; then I perceived that the wood was echoing back his
music, and that he believed himself con-
fronted with a mocking rival. For three
or four minutes the singing was kept up
without a break. Then the bird ceased,
giving his rival an opportunity to set the
tune. There was unbroken silence in the
wood, and in a little while the bird began
again, sounding his cry some ten or a dozen
times. He paused again; then, finding his
enemy still refused to sing a song of his
own setting, he uttered a solitary bell-voiced
"Cuckoo!" and was silent—perhaps triumphantly, but rather, I believe, with a clear
sense of having played the fool in trying
conclusions with a simple echo.

# On Sunday Morning

I bethought me of an episode observed the day before upon the towans : wide spaces of reed-grown sand that line the coast a few miles west of the place where I was now walking. At first there was silence, only made more evident by the clamour of innumerable skylarks lost in the blue. Then I heard the note of a cuckoo just ahead ; in a moment the two big birds rose from among the reed-like " spire-grass." I had come near a railway-line that traverses the waste.

The hen-bird manifested a preference for the telegraph-posts and insulators, the cock posed on the wires a few yards behind her, and cuckooed with a sort of uncomfortable cheerfulness, his wings drooped, his tail absurdly cocked into the air. Presently he rose and flew onwards, inducing the hen to leave her resting-place and take the next post to that she had been occupying. Again he wooed her with song and amorous posturing ; again he lured her onward yet another stage. It was as though he would play the fairy prince, and convoy her into some Paradise of Birds. And though she made pretence of maintaining the proper feminine attitude, it was evident she had felt the magic of his call.

Such trifles filled the time until I had

reached the environs of the town ; then, I
will confess, I walked more briskly, and
with a guilty consciousness of my late occupation. For it was Sunday morning, and
the good people had already attended the
first of the Sunday's services—the seven
o'clock " class meetings "—so that they
looked askance upon me who had obviously
had no such admirable purpose in rising
early. And, if I was not greatly troubled
by their manifest disapproval, I had a
devouring appetite for the breakfast I knew
to be awaiting me.

# IN THE MARSHES

# IN THE MARSHES

It was little enough to be thankful for: only a single shower while two friends sat together after midnight at a window overlooking the sea. One lounged at ease, playing a host of foolish ditties in a sort of whisper on his banjo; he did not conceal his amusement when presently his companion leant backwards out of the window that he might feel the fall of the rain on his face. But the shower was all too quickly over: they rose and filled their pipes. "Shall we go out?" said one, and in a moment they were traversing the one long street of the little town.

All things had now the breathing quietness of a pleasant sleep; the air was exquisite in its unaccustomed moistness, and the sea hushed and soothed the world of mortals to forgetfulness of all care. Very soon the spirit of the night imposed itself even upon these, the last waking souls of the village. They returned, and, once

they were abed, sleep came most naturally,
unwooed ; waking full early they enjoyed
a sense of having dreamed and forgotten a
multitude of pleasant dreams.    As thus :

> "The wind came whispering in the night ;
> Then, soft against my window-pane,
> Followed the murmur of the rain,
> And O, my love, my heart was light ;

> " For, sure, this promise stood confest :
> That soon yourself would come again,
> Who sent cool winds and welcome rain
> From out your kingdom of the West.

> " So I kept vigil all the night
> While still the rain fell whisperingly ;
> I dared to dream you dreamt of me,
> And O, my love, my heart was light."

Their occupation that day in a neighbouring tin-mine pleased and could not tire
them ; and, though it was raining when
they came again to the surface, the clouds
did but lend necessary contrasts of shadow
to a sunny landscape when they had changed
to everyday clothing and dined at the
'count-house with the "cap'n."

In the fields, as they went homeward,
it was hot enough to make an easy saunter
the only method of progression.    To one
of the two there is a potent charm in the
very name of "elder-blowth ;" and here
was elder-blowth in plenty.    For the dis-

trict is chiefly productive of broccoli, and prudent farmers divide and subdivide the fields with elder hedges for the protection of their crops. Even now there was a good wind : the bay was filled with long white breakers, and all the coast, from the Cuddan to Lamorna, was outlined with tossing foam.

So the two came very slowly, prying into all the secrets of the hedgerows, enlightening one another on the simpler mysteries of human nature, down upon the back of the village. For each there were letters waiting in the room that looks on the sea ; and presently they were abroad again and making for the Marshes.

After all, the reed that remains a reed in the river has but small excuse for regretting that the choice of Pan fell not upon it. For (to begin) supposing the god to be duly careful in the choice of his material, it must be granted he is strangely careless in its subsequent manipulation : so that often of a good reed he makes an indifferent flute. Now a man is always a man, and, like the reeds in the river, retains at least his birthright ; but what a misfortune for one who should have been a poet to be but a poetaster ! The reeds, again, have the same gift of whispered music, whether the wind come softly or lustily from east or west ; but when Pan has ennobled the reed of his choice it is voiceless in itself and can but pray to be delivered from the hands of the unskilled musician.

It is, best, in fine, to have the gift of taking things as they are, of enjoying the common gifts of nature.

There was one, not long ago, who walked the Marshes in a perpetual passion of disgust. He would grant that the place had still a certain quality of loveliness, but (being a painter of landscapes) he found that beauty lamentably diffused, and could say little in praise of a country that did not divide up spontaneously, as it were, into little subjects for his art. Also, they had been draining the marshes, insidiously robbing them of their peculiar charm. The painter railed at the idiocy of the world in general, and made a business of damming the obnoxious dykes ; he would tip a turf into a new-made channel with the air of a Guido Fawkes. To walk here was thus for him a tremendous exercise of the temper, very indifferently performed.

But the two who had come here this evening were merely human. They had set forth with a resolve of enjoyment, in itself a sufficient guarantee of felicity. They were in the mood to laugh at the painter's impassioned cry, "It doesn't compose!" Indeed, it was the very charm of the place that its beauty was rather felt than visible.

Before the Marshes are reached a stream flows under an old grey bridge to the sea. Doubtless it is innocent of fish ; it is shallow, narrow, and flows between banks low and unadorned. But here, in the moment of extinction, it is also for a moment glorified. For the banks and the ground thereby are literally carpeted with sea-pinks, growing in crowded companies, and not—as on the cliffs—in separate clumps. The two loitered here awhile, and then tracked the stream into the marsh.

It betokens a mind hopelessly prejudiced when a man is found to cry out against the railway as destructive of all natural beauty. To be away from the noisy world is happiness ; yet does a man need occasional reminders of his blessedness. The marsh is traversed throughout all its length by the main line of the Great Western, and now and again these idlers paused to watch a passing train. It was a pure delight to consider, when the train had passed and disappeared, how little this intrusion of the outside world had been able to affect their kingdom of quiet.

Over on the eastern slope of the valley a dog barked vehemently, collecting a great company of sheep and urging them to where the shepherd waited in the twilight, leaning on an open gate.  Here again the two paused : it was indeed the sole object of their expedition to find excuses for loitering.  Before them was a veritable "plain of reeds;" a space of marshy ground all overgrown with horsetails that to this day (as one remembers them) will not resolve themselves into a simple mass of colour, but remain a vast assemblage of green lines separately quivering.  Beyond these were tracts of taller flags, whose exquisite soft green made beautiful by contrast the crude yellow of innumerable blooms.

Now and again a blackbird shrieked in flight, and one sang steadily out of an elder-bush that glimmered dusky-white beyond the flags.  Over in the west the last faint gold of sunset showed on soft grey clouds, deliciously ominous of rain.

There were attempts at conversation, but the one was moved to talk of past adventures while snipe-shooting in the Marshes, his companion found the subject

# In the Marshes

unworthy. He, upon the other hand (since the stream is over-wide for jumping and bridged infrequently), dragged the unhappy sportsman full a mile, lest there should remain a shadow of doubt as to whether a patch of creamy white, seen from a distance of thirty yards, was in truth mountain bedstraw.

Yet, a little later, when it was beyond doubting that a certain bush held a nest of some sort, they did but linger a moment and pass on without making any search. For they had forgot their skill in birds'-nesting, and realised that their happiness would be lost did they permit themselves to look for that they were not well assured of finding.

And yet . . . . I believe they talked light-heartedly enough as they turned and made for the village, and that each had occasion to wonder yet again at the other's easy knowledge of the world and its inhabitants. But once there came a heavy sigh, immediately upon the heels of an apostrophe to the scene's loveliness ; and, if I mistake not, one of the twain was conscious all the while of certain lines that would repeat themselves audibly within him : " Never the time and the place, and the loved one altogether ! " Any loved one would have done ; but it was an outrageous thing that here and at such a season a man should be limited to a man's companion-ship.

Usually, I conjecture, these twain would have been proud to boast their freedom ; but a man is the child of many genera-tions, so that his instincts (voices of dead ancestors) condemn him loudly if he refuse, or is unable, to occupy himself at a given season as they direct. Surely it was for some such reason that the wanderers drifted into silence, as if each began to discover folly in the egregious wisdom of his com-rade ?

And who shall wonder that presently the banjo found for the first time an unkindly critic, and could keep neither player nor listener from his bed ?

# INTERLUDES

# INTERLUDES

## I—THE OFFERING

It was a hateful Spring. A dry wind came continually out of the east; the sun blazed on the parched fields; the very primroses were slack and curled at the edge. There was no moisture in the air, and no refreshment. Even sleep brought little comfort, and sleep was well-nigh impossible to man.

All through the morning, and far down the afternoon, I had been wandering after certain folk who were vaguely held to live somewhere within an area of five square miles. I had questioned stupid rustics, and proved unable to convince them that I was neither a bum-bailiff nor the agent of some swindled tradesman. I had found no trace of those I sought, and a fierce irritation arose in me against the friends who had sent me forth on this fool's errand.

There was a high wall on my right: built, they say, by one resolved to prove to a lying country-side that he had money as well as barren acres; who therefore spent thousands of pounds in works whereof there was manifestly no need. On the other side were stone-faced hedges, topped with gorse, brambles, and broom; the primroses lolling limply to the dust along their base.

The irritation grew as I traversed the endless way.

Presently there was a break in the wall: I had come to the first lodge, and half a dozen children were playing about the gate. I passed on, scarce seeing them. Then a little voice was raised. I looked back. A small child, yellow-haired and with the sunniest smile, had run after me a little way, and now paused, half adventurous and half afraid, in the middle of the roadway. " Hullo! " she cried.

" Hullo! " I answered, carelessly.

Then the others hailed me in a shrill chorus. " Hullo! " they cried; and again I answered them.

" Maister! " called the first.

I looked back again. " Will 'ee have a daffodil? " she asked; and then I saw that each of the six children carried a daffodil, doubtless a part in the ceremonial of some game. I thanked the child; she advanced, and held the flower at arm's length, and when I had taken it I was about to retreat. But again I was arrested. "Maister!" cried five shrill voices in chorus. And, when I had stopped and turned : "Will 'ee have a lily?"

Again I thanked them, and they came forth and surrendered the flowers, some boldly enough, and some very timidly, as if in awe. Then they ran back to the plat of gravel before the lodge-gate, and stood watching until I turned the corner.

I know not what change had come over me. I walked with twice the energy. Presently, when a shaggy cart-horse, of ineffable age, looked at me across a gate, I turned aside and lingered. It was a real disappointment that he would not allow himself to accept the kindness I intended.

In a moment, seeing that the daffodils were wholly faded and had broken stems, I flung them over the hedge, and went forward swiftly along the dusty road.

# II—THE HAMMOCK

THE creeping shadows grew longer on the rough grass of the orchard, and it was cool at last. I do not think I slept : the blessed quiet of the place was a thing to be tasted and enjoyed, and not forgotten. Yet, though I might survey the full approach from the house, it was not until the hammock began to sway gently that I knew myself no longer alone. The consciousness of this movement dawned upon me slowly, and with it came a little voice, crooning certain foolish songs with an exquisite tenderness.

I peeped warily.

The fair-haired baby (she can scarce be four) stood on a stool to swing me. She was still singing softly to herself, and as I watched I knew that, sleeping, I was a child to the mother in her ; and, seeing her face so gravely tender, I no longer wondered that the freakish creature should be thus supremely content, but almost held my breath, lest I should awaken the child in her again.

Once, indeed, I thought that it was over. Looking about her, she had espied the hoard of fruit that lay betwixt two cabbage-leaves upon the grass hard by. She stepped from her stool, and she forgot her song; she raised the upper leaf and surveyed my raspberries with a face of the most wicked delight. But the smile faded; it passed even while her fingers dallied with the fruit.

She rose, replaced the leaf, and came again to the side of the hammock; and now the low stool satisfied her no more. Still infinitely careful not to break my sleep, she replaced it with so high a chair that, when she stood upon it, her face was a little above the level of my own. She was singing again, but in the softest whisper, and her look had a sweet seriousness. With a strange definiteness of purpose she smoothed my rumpled hair, and altered the fall of my coat.

Then she was quiet, and stood regarding me with such a look that I could have believed her skilled to heal all pains by the mere power of sympathy. Last of all, she bent over and kissed me, her soft lips falling light and cool as the touch of the morning wind on one that has watched down the night. I saw her face, and it wore that aspect of grave happiness you have found in the looks of people coming from some sanctuary. And in a moment she stepped lightly from the chair and went across the grass.

I was loth to admit the play was ended.

I waited, with the hope that she would still come back. But soon it was clear she had forgotten. "Hullo, Trix!" I cried.

She turned. Her small face gleamed with wickedness and laughter, as a brook gleams that spreads itself over its pebbles in sunlight.

"Hullo, Stupid!" she cried. "Get out and swing me."

THEY had kindled huge wood fires on all the wide hearths of the transmogrified farmhouse, and for awhile it seemed well that they should have done so. The New Year had but just opened, and the warm blaze seemed to suit the season. But the old house lies in the West Country, and presently the warmth grew excessive. The moonlight was shining on the sea, and making black shadows round the dazzling quartz-gravelled paths of the garden. The man had flung open the window of a little deserted room to which he had wandered with Jessica, and the air was like Spring's own.

They stood silently for a moment. Then, "Your flowers are dead of the heat," he said, "come out and I will gather you a rose."

"But they are dancing still," said Jessica. "I believe I promised . . . ."

"Forget your promises," he answered. "Come out."

" The garden looks beautifully cool," she murmured, with a little pretence of hesitation.

"We can go without being noticed," said the man. " Come along." And as Jessica made no reply, he led the way into the garden.

The moon was full, and the yellow lights that dotted the sea were fainter and more mysterious than they would have been on a darker night. They went bareheaded down the gravelled pathway, and looked out over the quiet village without speaking.

"You promised me a rose," said Jessica, presently.

" There was a lovely Gloire de Dijon under the library window this morning. Let us go and find it."

Now the library was the room in which the others were dancing, and though a pistol shot without had hardly reached their ears amid the merriment of the dance, the two moved warily in the moonlight, and Jessica stood like a guilty person as he stepped across the narrow bed to pick the rose that bloomed there in the shadow.

" Poor flowers !" she murmured when he came back to her side, and she looked down at the faded roses at her breast.

"They were beautiful this morning. This air should revive them."

There was a little pause, the man standing with his newly plucked flower in his hand. Then Jessica took the withered flowers from her breast, and bent down as if to lay them on the soft brown earth. "They will be glad to die out here in the air," she said.

But the man interrupted, touching her on the shoulder. "You might give me one of them now that they are dead," he said.

"But——"

"O! you will only be giving me back my own. Did you not know?"

Jessica hesitated, and played with the withered roses that lay in her hand. "How should I know?" she asked at last. "They came without a name."

"But you guessed?" he persisted. "And now you will give me one of them?"

"Yes," said Jessica, "I guessed—and of course I will give you back one of your own, if you wish it."

So the exchange of flowers was made, and the man stored his in his pocket, while the one that he had newly gathered replaced the gift he had sent her in the morning, knowing they were to meet at night. Then he seemed about to say something, and a little at a loss for words. Indeed, he had not spoken when Jessica started and turned from him.

"Listen!" she said. "All the others are coming out. They must have missed us."

There are times when the lowliest counts himself the centre of the whole wide world, and Jessica's supposition was not, perhaps, without a certain justification. But it was quite unfounded: the absence of these two truants had passed unnoticed, and it was only the beauty of that temperate winter night and the warmth of the room that had brought them into the open air.

They came out in a body, and then the two watchers saw little groups detach themselves and go in divers directions. Presently a number of the intruders came laughing and talking towards them.

"What shall I tell them?" asked the man, suddenly, with a new meaning in his voice.

"What do you mean?" asked Jessica, a little puzzled.

But the man had stepped forward, and she saw his face clearly in the moonlight. She had no need to question farther.

"Tell them — tell them whatever you like," she said shyly. Then she stood waiting in the shadow, while he stepped forward gladly to meet his friends.

# IV—THE BLESSING OF THE RAIN

I sat, most miserable, in a room that opened on the garden. The nightingales were singing and, if ever I listened, a little wind was moving among the leaves ; but the heat lay heavy upon the land, and the parched earth had no nutriment to give to flowers or fruits, nor any comfort to men.

It was already after midnight. I had spent more than an hour in wretched meditation upon the events of the evening. Phyllis was here in the house—Phyllis, who had been wont to bring with her the very breath of the Spring when she came in Winter out of the West—and because of some word spoken or left unspoken she had cried impatiently that she would be better away, and I had half admitted to myself that she spake truly in her anger.

Doubtless she was sleeping now, and had forgotten that which kept me miserably awake. In the morning, perhaps, it would seem to her that the thing had never come to pass : I, also, it might be, should be unable to convince myself of its reality. But, in the meantime, the thought of sleep was altogether beyond me because of the intolerable heat ; and our little quarrel seemed a thing irremediable and not to be forgotten.

The nightingale stopped singing as if entranced by some "unheard melody" more sweet than the songs of his rivals who had kept him active hitherto. The very wind was silent for a space, and then it returned with a sudden increase of impulse. There was a sound as of the pattering of the feet of all Titania's host among the leaves, the whispering of their voices as they advanced to some high festival. Everything was changed in all the world, for this was the sound of the rain that was come again.

The magic of it wrought upon me with no more delay than came between the hearing of the sound and its interpretation. I rose from the place where I had been sitting, and crossed the room to the open French window. The rain was falling in good quantity, and the wind drove it pleasantly against my face. The stars were veiled, and the air had all it had lacked for so long a time.

# Interludes

I stood at the window looking out into the gloom of the garden. Stray drops of the rain fell on face and hands at intervals, and it was these that changed so utterly the complexion of my thoughts. I knew that in the morning the foolish quarrel of the night would be clean washed away, even as the dust would be washed from the leaves of the garden, and the lovely greenness shown that the drought had not yet ruined. We could afford some mortal weaknesses, Phyllis and I, since there was that between us no mortal chances could avail to break.

I was glad now to think she was sleeping, though I knew that in the morning she would envy me these first moments of the fall of the rain. At last I grew tired of my station. The exquisite dusk of the garden tempted me, and I stepped out to wander under the giant beeches along its gravelled pathways.

I came at last—as perhaps I had known I should come when I entered the garden —to the path beneath her window, and the words of a half-forgotten poem came back to me :

> " Beating heart, we come again
> Where my love reposes. . . . ."

I could not but remember the rest of the

verses, albeit well aware that she must be sleeping. And while I envied the man in the poem a lovely miracle happened, for Phyllis spoke to me out of her window framed with roses.

"Is it you?" she cried softly, bending forward, so that I saw the pale face dimly.

"I could not sleep," I answered. "I did not think you would be still awake."

"I was unhappy," she said, "until——"

"The rain has come," I interrupted. "You will be more contented now?"

There was something of a pause. "Yes, I am happy enough now. And you?"

"O," I said, "I am the happiest man in the world. The rain works wonders."

"It has been known to work most cruelly upon those who walk in it bareheaded," she said. "It was foolish of you to sit up so late. You should have been sleeping long ago. Good-night."

"Good-night," I said; but still it did not occur to me to turn into the house and seek my bed. The rain was not less delicious than it had been at first.

"Are you not going?" she asked.

"It is so pleasant here," I said, "that even the best of dreams would be a poor exchange for these realities."

"But think of the morning!" she cried.

# Interludes

" I shall be in the garden very early. You should have been sleeping long ago." There was a sudden stir among the net of branches round the window, and then a rose fell at my feet. "Good-night," she cried softly.

"Good-night," I answered, and as I stooped to take her gift I was aware of the nightingale, singing again with a new rapture, as if in gratitude for the blessing of the rain.

# V—THE UNSEEN SINGER

I was alone in the little seaside town, the solace of work denied because of the illness that had brought me there. For a year past I had longed for a period of licence such as was now mine, but the granting of my desire had come in such a fashion that it gave no pleasure. I was desperately tired, and my nerves in a state that rendered all enjoyment impossible. I used to lie late in the mornings, for there was nothing to do but wander idly on the promenade, and the trivial pleasures of the crowd vexed me unutterably because I could not share them. It was only at night I realised that possibly this irksome time of rest was bringing me nearer recovery. Then I used to wander until all but the latest of the visitors had left the promenade. It was impossible not to be at rest. The coolness of the night, the soothing murmur of the sea, and the shining yellow lights of a fishing village across the bay, combined to make a perfect world, and as I watched I knew that even the garish day might some day give me pleasure again.

I had been perhaps a fortnight in the place when first I saw the lady of whom I would tell you. It was only for a moment, as she drove past in the company of an older woman, but that moment's sight was enough to fill my thoughts until I saw her again upon the morrow. She was beautiful beyond all words : I fancied she could hardly have passed the age of twenty, and speech and hearing had been denied her. She had the innocent gladness that remains while they are yet young with some who are thus afflicted. She looked upon the world with beautiful bright eyes, and, in despite of fate, was well pleased to be alive. But she was talking with her fingers to the elder lady, her companion, in whose eyes as they looked on the girl I beheld an infinite pity.

That pity invaded my own heart instantly, though its object was gone out of my sight within a few seconds of her appearance, despite the fact that I knew not so much as her name, there was mixed with it a sense of angry rebellion against the fates who had thus afflicted her, wantonly robbing of its value a generosity that, through her, might otherwise have gladdened the wide world. I could not refrain from laughter at the emotions so suddenly aroused in me. I might have been her lover, and this inability to hear or to speak a calamity quite newly fallen upon her.

Now, more than ever, I regretted my loneliness, for I had no one from whom I might expect to gather any information, nor was there a hope of my gaining the privilege of her acquaintance. I made some futile inquiries at the hotel, and only got so far as to be almost certain she was, like myself, a visitor.

On the next day, at about the same hour, the carriage passed along the length of the promenade. She was still innocently glad to be alive, content to accept her burden as if it were no burden at all : it was with smiles she looked into the pitying eyes of her companion, and I could fancy that the messages she was conveying with swiftly moving fingers were humorous appreciations of what she saw around her.

My earlier questions had been addressed to a quaint, elderly waiter at the hotel : a man who had in some sort made it his special task to see to my well-being, and who was the nearest approach to a friend

I possessed within a hundred miles of the place. It happened that I was lunching at the open window one day when the carriage passed a little earlier than usual.

" That is the lady of whom I was speaking," I said to him.

He looked out of the window with quick interest. " A dear little maid, if I may say so. Iss, and the poor dear is deaf and dumb : she's talkin' upon her fingers. Well, I thought from what you told me they must be strangers in these parts, and so they are. I don't even know the horses nor the carriage."

Thus passed a period of several days. I began to find myself vastly better, and, with the growth of energy, to look forward pleasurably to the time when I should return to my work in London. My good friend the waiter had succeeded, much to his delight, in getting me to go for numerous drives through the lovely country that surrounds the watering-place. I had even, on divers occasions, set forth on foot and explored the coast and the inland lanes for myself. I went alone, but I never felt the absence of companions, for my expeditions always took place before or after the hour at which she might be expected to pass along the promenade, and so my thoughts were always busy, whether with anticipation or remembrance.

Never once did she fail me ; never once did her affliction seem to mar the beautiful gaiety of her mood. It appeared that she saw and enjoyed every little thing that could be seen ; nor was it altogether a young man's vanity that made me wonder whether she had begun to notice the fact that a certain sallow invalid was always idling on the promenade at the hour when she drove by.

I had come to understand the routine of their daily outing. They were manifestly living somewhere to the west of the town. Every day they went through the inland lanes at the back of it until they were a mile or two to the east, and then, descending seawards, drove home by the promenade and the road that skirts the sea.

Now one day, with no set purpose that I would have confessed, even to myself, I took the western road and went into the country. The road lies for some distance between low hills and the southern sea : at first the sun's heat was intolerable, but gradually one mounted higher, and then the sunlight was but the fit accompaniment of the lively wind that blew in from the sea. So I went forward in the best of spirits until I had come to the edge of a great valley that runs inland from the sea.

Some dozen or so cottages and a little pier stood at the margin of the sea. Inland a few houses were seen among their fruitful orchards. But at the edge of the slope there was a little space of wild wood, and this, as I looked across the flower-grown hedge, tempted me to rest. I climbed the intervening barrier and lay down in the shelter of a little oak-tree. The sunlight flooded a wealth of bracken, foxgloves, and golden harvest-weed. I lounged at ease, content to watch stray butterflies that went lazily from flower to flower.

It may be I slept. Certainly I was a long time under the oak before I became aware that I was not the only occupant of the wood. Some one was singing softly, and I could hear footsteps moving slowly through the fern. I could tell by the sound that the newcomer was stopping here and there to pick flowers.

Now, I had enjoyed the solitude, but even at the first the person who was coming towards me did not strike me as an intruder. Her singing was in absolute concord with my mood : it was as if one had thought of a poem and a moment later found oneself humming the melody that would make of it a perfect song. I lay and waited, and the singer came nearer.

The song ceased when she presently appeared. She was a little startled, but not near so much as I.

"Then you are not dumb!" I cried involuntarily, as I started to my feet.

She hesitated, and a little smile played about the corners of her pretty mouth. "It is my aunt who is dumb," she said. Then, with a sudden recovery of her dignity, "I don't know why you should ask."

But that was a matter I had no great difficulty in explaining.

# MIDSUMMER MOONLIGHT

# MIDSUMMER MOONLIGHT

I HAD worked long and late. Now at night there was no resisting the call of the sea, which came so softly to my cottage in the coombe that I could have fancied the ancient hills whispered like a hollow shell. I lingered a little while in the garden that overhangs the dusty road; for the great bush of scented verbena planted against my window now spread an exquisite fragrance. In the very moment of my coming forth a last light vanished from the window of the farm-house over against my door; even in the village there were but few houses in which the folk had not retired.

The moon was up and near its full, but a thin mist had come up from the sea along with the rising tide, and, advancing, had enveloped the land. It had assimilated and absorbed the yellow radiance in such a fashion that the light seemed rather to be a quality of the atmosphere itself than to emanate from a material source. I drew in a great breath of the cool air; then I took the road to the sea.

It was very quiet. There was no sound beyond the gurgle of a stream that runs beside the road, and the sea's quiet breathing. Over on the western slope a corncrake sounded his grating note; but in the village all was quiet. Crossing the little bridge presently, and making westward to the cliffs, I found a single visitor smoking on the low parapet of granite. Then I went forward and took the rough path that leads into the wastelands.

On my right the tide had covered a huge level beach; and the white waves creamed and glimmered under the moonlight, until they were but ghostly mysteries moving vaguely in the gloom. Below, under the sheer cliffs, they broke strongly against black rocks, sending up luminous evanescent clouds of spray, and booming hoarsely around the walls of some deep-sunken cavern. It was a night when the commonest mortal might look to see white ghosts of beautiful unhappy ladies, such as he would pity greatly and fear not at all.

I went slowly along the pathway, a steep slope, clad in whispering heather, rising for a hundred feet above me, while on the

# Midsummer Moonlight

seaward side the cliffs fell sheer for twice that distance. Point after point, as I looked forward, loomed huge and black against the glimmer of the moonlight; there was no sign of life, no sound but the noise of the sea. It was as if the great earth slept and one heard the strong beating of its pulse. Gradually I shared in this delicious peace, breathing it in with the pleasant air, enveloped in it as by the thin luminous mist. I was abandoned to enjoyment of the night, and took no heed of how the time was flying.

Imagine, then, my emotions when this universal stillness was broken by a confused noise of distant shouting.

I stood and listened attentively. Suddenly the shouting ceased, and, looking up, I beheld the figure of a man outlined against the sky on the highest point of a headland before me. I confess the apparition somewhat disconcerted me; a moment later I was yet more amazed when I heard the thin sweet notes of a flute, and realised that this wanderer was playing antique dances, here on the cliffs, with only mermaids waking to hear.

I moved forward rapidly, intent on discovering the meaning of these eccentricities All at once the music ceased; and then, before one could count ten, the mermaids applauded their minstrel. That is to say, there came a sound of cheering, even of hand-clapping, out of the glamour of mist and moonlight that veiled the sea.

The musician waited until the sound had died away. Then he resumed his playing, with such an accession of spirit as showed he had found the applause invigorating. In a moment the pathway dipped, and he was hidden from my sight. The music was fainter now because of the rocky screen that parted us. It was with something like a renewal of my first surprise that I stepped out upon the headland, within a yard or two of his position.

He saw me and ceased to play. Recognising him, I wondered I had not known him by his music. But there was excuse for me : Josephus Pascoe is a man of the most rigid respectability upon all ordinary occasions, and had I not seen I could not have believed him capable of such a performance as this.

I stepped forward. "What, in the name of wonder, are you up to ?"

He stared at me through the moonlight. "You, sir ?" he said, with an evident relief. "Did 'ee fancy I was playin' for the piskies? Well, they say 'tis here they've got their gardens to this day, **if only a** man had the proper eyes to **see** them with. Now, is that what **you** thought?"

Before I had had time **to** answer, a voice **came** hoarsely out of **the** sea. "Play up! Play up! 'Tis lonesome here, for all we're six **of us,** and the music **do keep** the **heart** in us."

Pascoe looked **at me.** "Do 'ee know now who they be I'm playin' for?"

"Hardly," I said. "Though I swear they **are no piskies.**" And immediately he turned **and looked** seawards.

"Ahoy, there!" he **shouted.** "Who be 'ee?"

There was a momentary pause. "We be three young chaps **from** over **to** Porth, **and a** maid with **every one** of us."

"**Where** be 'ee **to?**" shouted **Pascoe.**

"**Why out** 'pon **the Gull Rock, to be** sure," answered his invisible interlocutor, **seeming to** grow a little **angry** at this cate-chism.

"**And what be** 'ee doin' **out** there?" continued Pascoe, relentlessly.

"Why, freezin' with **the** cold!" came the answer, very brusquely; and then Pascoe turned to me.

"I was comin' **from over** to Porth just **before** you met **me,** an' I had my flute with

me for company; the cliffs is lonely, even
when 'tis moonlight. However, I was
happy enough, blowin' away 'pon it as I
walked along, when all at once I heard
some one shoutin' at me out of the sea.
The heart of me stood still: I was stiff
with fright. But I took courage in the
end. 'Ahoy, there!' I shouted, 'Who be
'ee?' and the answer came, same as you
heard: 'We be three young men from
over to Porth, and a maid with every
one of us.' After that I could see there
was nothing to frighten a man. So I asked
more questions, and, come to think upon it,
you don't know all the story yet."

Once again he turned towards the sea,
where the black mass of the Gull Rock
loomed ghostly in the mist. "Ahoy, there!"
he shouted. "However do 'ee come to
be 'pon the Gull Rock at this time o'
night?"

The man on the Gull Rock had fairly
lost patience. "How do 'ee think we come
to be here? Didn' I tell 'ee we came out
in George Penhalurick's boat, and the
darned thing drifted away after we landed,
three hours ago? Play up, man; we're
freezin' with the cold."

Pascoe looked at me as he fingered the
flute. "'Tis a lovely night, and I'm in no

# Midsummer Moonlight

great hurry for my bed, so I said I'd give
them a tune for company."

He turned away and straightway began
to play, choosing a certain antique tune
that would set frail octogenarians dancing if they chanced to be of Cornish
blood.

It was, indeed, a marvellous night, and
to think of sleep was impossible.  A pretty
madness inspired the whole adventure.  I
was well content at first to be an idle by-
stander, paying no heed to the dictates of
common sense.  But a breath of cold air
came from the sea, and, shivering, I threw
off the influence of the moonlight.

"Joe," I said, for so his name is vulgarly
abbreviated, "your music is delightful; but
do you think they'll care to listen until
morning?"

The flute dropped from his hands; he
faced me with amazement written on every
feature.  "Where was my senses?" he
asked.  "I never thought of that.  Why,
they'll be starved with the cold."

He turned towards the prisoners: "Boys!"
he shouted, "you must keep up heart without the music.  I'll go in to Trelorne as
quick's I can, and in half an hour we'll
have 'ee off in a boat.  So long to 'ee till
then!"

# Midsummer Moonlight

He stooped, picked up his flute, and stowed it in his pocket after a careful wiping. Then he set forth along the path in such a haste that, following, I wished well I had held my peace.

# A WAYSIDE EVANGELIST

# A WAYSIDE EVANGELIST

I was sick of breathing the used-up air of London, the air whose contact fouls and not cleanses ; for a little while the train that sped towards the country seemed instinct with the home atmosphere whereinto it should carry me. But the day was parching hot, and the stink of the engine-smoke was everywhere.

One might let down the windows to the full ; the fields were green without, and presently we had sight of a shining blue sea, with gulls floating white above it as far as the horizon. But still the compartment retained its own particular atmosphere : the atmosphere of London. The fields, the hills, the valleys where the trout stream glittered through the leafage, were the incarnation of beauty and of quiet, but the sight of them conferred no mitigation of discomfort. Surely to souls in purgatory there could be nothing more intolerable than the slow passage before their eyes of a panorama revealing all the unattainable beautiful places of the earth?

Only one thing was possible : to long, as the sick long for sleep, for the end of the journey, the scent of elder in the fields, and the air that comes clean-washed from the sea. And at last, even as the sick sleep before the dawn, we had reached the home-place, and were free of the little ugly town. And in this first hour there was no man in all the streets whose voice and familiar accent did not give him the aspect of an old friend suddenly come upon.

And later, to go forth from the houses and gain the fields that lie along the cliffs, shut in by hedges of flowering elder : to breathe the soft, grey air from the sea : it was a death to the heat and worry of London, a new birth unto cleanliness—of body, it seemed, no less than of spirit. The dew stood as of old, a dust of grey drops, upon the grasses.

And for sheer gladness of heart, and because it was good to loiter, I was fain to address an aged farmer who laboured near the pathway, putting in broccoli among the withered stalks of newly drawn potatoes.

I was smoking a cigarette.

# A Wayside Evangelist

"Well, farmer," I said. "How does the weather suit you?"

The old man looked up over his shoulder without a word. Then something in my aspect seemed to take his attention. "Well, stranger," he said. "I should like for you to tell me what you do smoke bacca for?"

I laughed, flicking the ash from my cigarette. "Oh!" I said, "because I like it, I suppose."

The old man stuck his long-handled shovel into the ground, resting one foot upon the shoulder of the blade, and using the handle as a staff. He looked at me with the smile of one too old in this world's ways to be fooled like a child with reasons that were no reasons.

"Do 'ee mean to tell me that's a reason for usin' bacca : that you'd like it? An' you d' look a rais'nable 'nough man, too."

"I hope so," I answered. "Pretty much as God made me."

"Iss," he said. "Iss. An' some day you'll come to consider what use you've made o' what He made 'ee. But let that pass. Do 'ee mane t' tell me 'tis good for a man—body or soul—to waste time an' money smokin' bacca? Can 'ee give me wan raison, more 'n that you do like it?"

" Upon my soul," I said, " I can think of none. I have never sought for one. 'Tis enough that I like it."

He shook his head, sorrowful and yet amused. "Ah!" he said. "You'd like it!" He found my attitude merely pitiable.

Now a man can stand a good deal, and a joke is a joke, be it never so clumsy. But one grows tired at last of hearing one's sweetheart abused, though it be done most delicately, and in the merest jest. It is the same with tobacco.

" Come," I said, " you are surely wasting breath. 'Tis a vice, perhaps, as vice goes with some people ; but surely only a little one ? And are you so certain it is a vice at all ? The Lord made me "—the old man nodded slowly, his lips compressed, his eyes triumphantly eloquent of a coming rejoinder that should crush me—" and upon my honour he gave me a most exorbitant affection for tobacco. Also, he made the world, and with it tobacco——"

The old man's mouth opened as with the sudden release of a spring. His foot came down upon the shovel, driving it still deeper into the soil. He relinquished his hold upon the handle, and stood before me the very incarnation of triumph.

# A Wayside Evangelist

" No, He dedn'!" he cried. " No, He dedn'!"

His mouth closed smartly on the words. He dared me with his eyes to question his speech.

" But surely," I said, " surely He made the world?"

" To be sure," said my friend, with a nod of acquiescence.

" And all that therein is—tobacco?"

Once again the old man broke out upon me. " No, He dedn'! No, He dedn'!"

" Then where on earth, or out of it, did tobacco come from?" I asked with a certain desperation.

The old man looked upon me kindly. " You may depend, young man, the Lord wouldn' never be the author of anything that is evil under the sun. The fact is: bacca, like many other things, is a plant o' Satan's sowin'. Now, if you could give me satisfaction that bacca was growed in the Garden o' Paradise, you should smoak s' much's you mind to. I wouldn' say no more."

" Well," I said daringly, " I can give you no proof, but I take it no proof is wanted. How else does it get here?"

The old man came closer.

" My son," he said, " you may be saved,

you may be unsaved ; but, saved or unsaved, you can't believe the Lord would make evil things. Where do bacca come from ? Why, where do sin come from, an' drink, that do send men quick into Hell ? Why, Satan made them, o' course. Satan made them."

He paused a moment, surveying me with the very look of wise old age that would fain open the eyes of youth to the real meaning of things, yet remembers that in youth a certain ignorance is by no means to be accounted sin. Then he lifted up his voice :

"The Lord made man and woman to live together an' love one another, an' bring forth children, as is proper. But first he made a garden for them to live in. Now, do 'ee think there was weeds in it, an' slugs, an' snails, an' a passel of ol' brembles for to tear the clo'es off their backs ? No such thing ! There was apple-trees there, an' pears an' mazzards, an' all sorts of vegetables that's good for the soul o' man. An' doubtless there was roses, an' sweet Williams an' such-like, for Eve to tend 'pon times.

"But there was no weeds, an' no brembles, for the Lord couldn' make evil not ef He was to try, no more 'n a grey-bird could

# A Wayside Evangelist

caw like a crow. You may depend they would turn to flower or fruit, an' we should still know where they come from, an' bless the Giver.

"But Satan came, an' there was Eve ready to hand, an' Satan tempted her, an' from that moment 'twas all up with Adam. An' they went forth out o' the Garden, an' the Lord cursed them because of their sinfulness. *In the sweat o' thy brow*, He said, an' sure enough in the sweat of his brow (or some one else's) has man ate his bread ever since. He might ha' had the world o' God's making : he chose t' see what fashion world Satan would give en. An' Satan's world is full o' many weeds ; wherever you d' teal wheat, instead o' the corn do come up the charlock. An' so 'tis all the time.

"A man must be hoein' weeds now, 'stid o' sittin' under a tree with his wife, praisin' God, an' waitin' for the crops to grow. Tha's how 'twas meant to be. But 'tis the part of the fool to say the Lord made weeds, an' such like. He couldn' do it. They'm all o' Satan's sowin' : bacca with the rest."

Now here the old man ceased from his discourse, and because my cigarette was burnt out, I flung it from me over the hedge of elder. The action gave him a flush of joy.

"Thraw en away!" he said. "Thraw en away. 'Tis a trap of Old Satan."

And, smiling, I turned away, leaving him to go back to his labours.

# PILCHARDS IN THE BAY

THE day was perfect; autumn once again asserted her pre-eminence among the seasons, and appeared—despite a chill north-easter—the one period wherein it is supremely possible to live. I had crossed the ferry near by Hayle Bar to the Towans, a tract of sandhills overgrown with turf that keeps perennially short and velvet-like, and with reedy, gray-green spire-grasses. Presently the sandhills gave place to ruder cliffs, and I struggled through a hazel thicket that covers the slope. For a space I turned aside to look at the wishing-well, where pins without number bore witness to the frequency with which the waters had been interrogated in the summer.

Finally, I was upon the open waste again, and found the "huers" watching for pilchards at the white house on Carrickgladden. The boats had been a week in pay, and throughout that period had taken up their allotted positions daily along

the cliff. The season for the coming of
the fish was now fully arrived; and on the
previous day there had been nought but
pilchards taken by the drift-boats that went
out after mackerel and herring. The shoals
abide only a short time within the limits of
the bay, and if they be not swiftly encircled
within the seine, they pass out westwards
—sweeping from the north-east around the
bay—and are lost to the fishermen of St.
Ives.

The huers, therefore, scanned the wide
bay with unflagging attention; though one
found time to discuss with a roaming
stranger the mysterious ways of God with
man, even while he watched for the appearance of the "shade upon the waters"
that would be the sign of a bank of fish.
The wind was unfavourable: it made a
turmoil of sand and rotted shale in the
shallow water along the beach, and brought
to these western shores a part of the red
hematite that—coming from the tin mines
—perpetually incarnadines a great tract of
water along the farther cliffs. These things
would render it all the more difficult for the
huers to detect the pilchards—should they
come—by their colour on the water; and,
having in memory the evil chances of recent
years, I only pitied them, and the seiners

who awaited their signals, as people un-
fortunate in expecting overmuch.

But in the afternoon, when there was
scarce half an hour to dark, there came a
sudden cry of "Heva!" from the white
house.

Instantly the seiners were on the move,
rowing their hardest in obedience to the
signals of the huers. Each of these held
in either hand a couple of iron rings of
about a foot in diameter, set crosswise
upon a short handle and covered with
cloth, so that they formed white balls,
easily visible from sea against the background of heather and sad-coloured grass.
In the old days, furze-bushes were used for
this purpose; and still, though the white
balls are common, you hear them speak of
the "bushes" of the huers.

The code of signals is sufficiently simple :
to send the boats east, for example, both
bushes are held downwards at arm's length
on the left (or western) side; then raised
at arm's length above the head on the
right. A single bush held in the right
hand and swung round in the fashion of
a wheel means "Let out the line;" and,
finally, to hold both at arm's length in
front, swing them downwards and around
over the head to the initial position, then

raise a foot or so and bring them emphatically down through the same distance, is to give the exciting order, " Shoot the seine."

The seineboat and the accompanying towboat have parted company; the line of corks begins to appear on the surface as the net is hurriedly shot. The huers are still waving their bushes—for the fish are invisible except from this height, and it is they who steer the boat—and shouting through huge speaking-trumpets instructions one must be a fisherman to interpret. At last the order is given to close the seine, and the towboat comes up with the stop-net.

While this is being let out and fastened, the men in the two boats are shouting and vigorously splashing their oars, intent upon driving the fish into the curve of the seine and away from its unsecured mouth. Meanwhile, the huers take breath, surveying the operations below. " Now bloucers ! " says one to the other; and immediately there goes forth landward from the two speaking-trumpets a great cry of "Bloucers! Bloucers!" that promptly summons the cobbler from his lapstone, the labourer from the fields, the very baker from his shop, to take part on shore in the securing of what the seiners have captured.

# Pilchards in the Bay

The seine was shot unusually late on this occasion—had but the fish come earlier there would have been two or three more seines shot, for there were other shoals about—and though the boat came in as soon as the net had been closed, it was dark when the warp reached the shore. This is a great rope, which is taken in hand by the bloucers and hauled up the steep beach, over the loose, dry sand, until it can be attached to one or other of the many capstans about the coast.

The one used was situated on a small plateau upon the face of the cliff, some forty yards above the beach. Hither came all the men of the neighbourhood, footing it delicately in the darkness over a narrow ledge sodden with the drainage of the hills, and here and there broken by a recent fall of the land.

The oldsters sat together under the cliff at the back of the ledge, talking philosophy. So long has ill-luck dogged them that their first effort was to put aside all natural hopes. "I don't take no account of it," said one. "Nor me," said another.

A third was lighting a pipe. "I'm got to that pitch," he said, when he had secured a light, "I don't put nothin' on it."

But somehow, though they never ignored

their duty of hoping nothing, one learned a good deal as to the benefits that might accrue to them if the seine should tuck well upon the morrow. In a little time the second warp was landed, to be connected with a second capstan : and by this means the great seine was slowly drawn inwards to such a position that even at high-tide it would still touch the bottom and afford no way of escape to the imprisoned fish.

The men worked bravely and with abundant cheerfulness ; but at the end of the evening one remembered chiefly this fact—that they were altogether prepared to find the seine near empty when the time came for "tucking," and had a dozen reasons for the catastrophe if upon the morrow it should be found to have happened.

All night the seiners watched by the net, a fire burning with cheerful radiance beneath the awning. The morning showed a sea so enveloped in fog that Godrevy lighthouse—a white tower on an island at the bay's eastern extremity—was scarce visible across the water from St. Ives ; and it was close upon eight o'clock before the cry of "Heva!" was heard again.

Meanwhile, the tuckers had long been

at work upon the first capture. Great
black boats, long past other service, were
dragged down by teams of four horses
from their accustomed resting-place and
towed out to the seine. A smaller net—
the "tuck-net"—was let down inside the
seine and closed ; then it was drawn to the
surface. The fish showed presently as a
boiling mass of silver ; or perhaps they
were more like molten tin when they
have plunged into it the sodden log
whose moisture, escaping, is to drive all
impurities to the surface-scum. The up-
flung scales and water stood for the spitting
of the metal.

The tuckers stood in their black barges,
dipping the fish out by the basketful, and
tipping them into the bottom of the boat.
Each boat contains when full somewhere
over thirty hogsheads—say one hundred
thousand fish—and yet in a very few
minutes the mass of madly moving silver
had risen to the knees of the men, who
stood away from the side and levelled it
with the edge of an empty basket, while
their companions in labour flung more and
more into the boat. Over the tuck-net
there was a continual flashing of silver
scales cast up, for the fish were well-nigh
solid in the net.

# Pilchards in the Bay

Now and again a stray fish, not yet within the tuck-net, came slowly towards the surface, too bewildered to be any longer susceptible of fear. The water, when the sun shone upon it, showed a clear green, spangled with innumerable scales; and at the line of corks which showed the limits of the seine you could see, looking down into the waters, thousands of pilchards lying dead in the folds of the net, like ingots of silver. There was endless shouting both of comradeship and criticism, and above all, the noise of these innumerable fish, struggling in heaps, and in the tuck-net at the surface.

Never a boat went by but had a hundred or two dying in its bows; and all around the central group of boats were men of enterprise who fished with long-handled nets for such fish as had died in the close quarters of the seine.

Meanwhile the huers had twice again raised their cry of " Heva," and so there were now three great seines in the water before St. Ives, in addition to that which was being tucked to the east, by Carrick-gladden.

Mounting to the hills above the water, one saw how it is that the presence of pilchards in the bay is detected by the huers ; for the fish had packed together in the deeper part of the seine, and showed a reddish black, like a sunken reef. At intervals they appeared to be seized with a sudden consciousness of their predicament, and the water boiled at the surface visibly.

On the previous day, and even this very morning, when there was light, it had been difficult for the unpractised eye to detect a sign before the net was closed ; and, indeed, the desultory talk of the bystanders was largely of historic occasions whereon a seine which had been shot in water deemed by the majority quite innocent of fish, turned out—to the glory of the huer who had seen the shoal—to be magnificently plenished.

It was good, too, to look back through a glass at the tucking of the first seine. The fog had changed to azure mist ; the sun shone brightly on a pale smooth sea, whose waves were little more than slowly moving lines of shadow. Seen against the level light, the boats and figures of the men were of a velvety blackness ; but the fish, as they struggled in the tuck-net or poured from the baskets into the boats, shone with an exquisite soft silveriness. And there the men laboured until the turn of the tide, when ten great boats, laden to the gunwale, were towed into the harbour, the further tucking of the seine being left until low water on some future day.

It remains to describe the scene in the harbour, whither the barges were towed, that the fish might be conveyed to the cellars and salted.

The boats were moored, and the carts backed into the water, where the horses stood most patiently—though with a certain look of dejection—while the fish were shovelled out.

The "jowsters"—men who retail the fresh fish throughout the neighbouring country—were buying their stock: his own particular business the one thing in the world to each. In the water and upon the grey sands a host of children wandered among their elders, the most having each separate finger thrust through the gills of a oilchard.

All the tidemark, also, was strewn with the fish, often near already, by reason of many trampling feet, to a condition of naked skeleton; and a great dogfish, caught and killed yestreen by one of the drift-boats, showed his white belly, rolling with the come and go of small waves : the only impassive thing in all the scene.

# Pilchards in the Bay

All the old men of the town were on the sands, uttering conjectures as to the probable number of hogsheads to be taken out of the seines, and enlarging upon the utter worthlessness of the most magnificent captures as prices are in these days. The reason of this falling-off is simple : there is no market, practically, for fresh pilchards ; they all go to the cellars, and thence to the Italian markets. Now, in the old time the Italians had to content themselves with Cornish pilchards, or be without fish of any sort; to-day, there is unlimited competition, and even the St. Ives' man realises that he will not choose "fairmaids" who can eat his fill of Newfoundland cod. Also, it is said, the Catholic religion loses its hold upon the people in those parts, and they scruple not to taste flesh on Fridays. It is a pity : eaten fresh, the fish is delicious ; and there are those who can stomach it when it has been salted. But in neither condition does it find a sale at remunerative prices.

The children, however, are bound to profit, and it is by no means the sons and daughters of the poor alone who descend to "cabing" as they name the practice of stealing fish from the boats or from the carts that convey it to the cellars. One man, manifestly of a temper not too well controlled, was followed at each journey by a score of urchins. Whenever his back was turned for a moment, one of the youngsters would dart forward and with one sweep of his hand send a score of pilchards flying out of the cart. His companions shouted exultantly as they scrambled for a share of the spoil; and the man, divided betwixt the care of his horse and of his load, swore impotently at them, or struck savagely at some daring boy. But his strength was spent upon the air, and the fish still came by hundreds out of his cart.

Finally, he must mount a steep and narrow lane betwixt two inns of immemorial fame, which are now annually compelled to find excuses for existence, such as will satisfy a hostile bench. The way was roughly paven; the fish came by dozens and half-dozens over the tail of the cart, and the children followed tumultuous, cabing now without fear of the driver's lash. When the ascent was made and the driver was at liberty to descend, they were already on their way to the beach again, looking for some new chance of plunder. There the labour of unloading ceases not, and already they are preparing for fresh ventures, if the fish come again.

# Pilchards in the Bay

One thing has in it, surely, the stuff of a picture worth painting. Down the grey granite quay, against the bluest of skies, march five-and-thirty tall and resolute fishermen in yellow oilers and great sea-boots. Each walks some three or four yards behind his leader; they bear upon their shoulders a great brown seine, which hangs in regular festoons between them. They are taking it from the cellar to their boat.

Night comes; the bay is filled with lights; and presently the drift-boats come back—their nets all empty—and the crews mingle with the rest. And thus by night and by day life takes its course with infinite picturesqueness in the little town, until, at the end of a week, nineteen hundred hogsheads of fish have been landed, and the seines are taken up. And indeed it is good to have shared this life, though merely as a spectator. For though the capitalist has possessed himself of the chief profits of this harvest, as of all others, the event is still for the good of all. For every hogshead of fish that has been taken, the bloucers will divide the sum of two shillings and tenpence between them; and the seiners and tuckers are paid good wages. There is no dweller in the neighbourhood who does not somehow share in the harvest of the sea ; and for twenty miles you will hardly find a cottage that has not its store of pilchards, purchased at any price from a shilling a hundred, and now put by in salt for winter use.   And, to conclude, these fishermen are of Nature's gentlefolk, and to have moved among them for a space is to have learned a lesson : of courtesy certainly, and perhaps also of patience.

# PAYMENT BY RESULTS

I can just mind my grandfather, and only just, for the old man died somewhere in the twenties, and I was no more than a small boy then. But I shall never forget the tale of how the tubs were found in his barn, and of how he escaped the fine. I seem to fancy that I heard him tell it when I was a little boy; I heard my father tell it once a week for thirty years; and I've told it more than once myself.

Well, in the year '4 my grandfather was living at Tregundy Farm, which lies a mile this side of Pentreath, to the right of the high-road. 'Twas a small place, but there was plenty of business doing then that you'd hardly find in *Farmer's Almanacks*, and so grandfather was reckoned pretty well off. To tell the truth, he had pretty much to do with the smuggling; and, indeed, 'twould have been hard for any man to keep out of it, considering the number of Pentreath boats that made the voyage over to Rusco' every month, and the profits of the traffic. Grandfather was churchwarden, I believe, and a big man in the place; but, nevertheless, on a certain Saturday, late in the year '4, he left more than a score of tubs of good liquor hidden under the straw in his barn, when he set forth upon the ten-mile ride into market.

Well, he rode in as usual and put up his horse at the "Godolphin." Then he took up his stand upon the causeway in front of the "Godolphin" door, along with half a hundred other farmers. He had dinner at the ordinary, along with the rest, and afterwards took his drop of toddy; then he came forth from the inn again and stood upon the step, looking up and down the street to see what was doing, before going across to old Lawyer Symons's upon some small matter of business. The clever-ness of that old man is not forgotten yet. though he's dead this sixty year. 'Twas well known that no case was too desperate for him to pull a man through. In the end he fell away through drink; he would sit in the "Godolphin" on market days watch-ing till some farmer came in for whom he had done business in bygone years. "Well, Mr. Thomas," he would say, "let me see: whose turn it is to stand treat to-day?" Of

course the farmer could take a hint like that. "Glass of the same," the lawyer would say; and sometimes he'd have half a dozen drops of gin standing in a line upon the mantelpiece. He was never known to refuse a drink—or to refrain from asking for one—because he hadn't finished the last. Ay, he fell away sadly, but he was a wonderful good lawyer in his time.

My grandfather stood upon the doorstep looking up the steep street, and meditating as to what he should say to the lawyer. Suddenly there was a noise in the distance. From the "Godolphin" step it was not possible to see much, for the road was lined on both sides with the standings of butchers, sweetsellers and so on. But in another minute my grandfather saw a horse come tearing down the street, and a little bit of a boy, bareheaded, and (as you might say) all blown to pieces, upon the back of it.

As soon as he saw the horse and the boy my grandfather's heart stood still; for 'twas his old grey mare, which had been on the farm for fifteen year, and the boy was the son of a neighbour who had had no small share in his smuggling ventures.

When the boy saw him he drew rein, and

tried to speak; but he couldn't fetch his breath.

"What is it?" cried my grandfather, stepping forth through the crowd that began to gather. "What's the matter? Thee's been and killed the old mare!"

At last the boy found breath to speak. "You was hardly gone out of sight when the riding-officers came, and made straight for the barn. They must have been told, for they found the kegs just as if a guide was with them. Missus sent me off at once upon the old mare to give 'ee warning, but you may depend the officers is after me, and not far off. You must do what you can, Missus said."

Grandfather heaved a great groan. "I'm a ruined man!" he said. "Clean ruined!"

There was a buzz of talk among the crowd which had gathered round him. "Iss!" said some one, "'Twould puzzle Lawyer Symons to save 'ee now."

Grandfather heard that, and he minded where he had been meaning to go before this news reached him; at least, he thought, he might as well go still. If there was a loophole Lawyer Symons was the man to find it.

Lawyer was a little small man, with a pink face, keen little blue eyes, and a

regular whirlwind of silver hair. Grandfather broke forth at once.

" Mr. Symons," he said, " I'm a ruined
man ! All the savings of fifty years are
gone. I shall end my days upon the
parish."

The lawyer looked at him without a
sign of surprise. " It must be bad trouble
that can't be mitigated," he said. " What
is gone wrong ? "

" What ? " cried my grandfather. " Why,
everything ! I'm a ruined man. There
was a few tubs of cognac in my barn this
morning when I came away. I was no
sooner out of sight than the riding-officers
came and found the lot of it. I shall be
exchequered in three times more than I'm
worth, and the end of it will be stark
ruin."

Still old Symons showed no signs of
being disturbed.

" Mr. Jeffrey," he said, " I did your
father more than one good service in his
time ; I fancy I've already been of use, in
one or two matters, to you. But do you
know what you have been doing this afternoon ? Do you know the office I have the
honour to fill ? "

My grandfather stared at him in a help-
less sort of way.

The lawyer rose and bowed across his table. "I have the honour to be one of the Commissioners of His Majesty's Exchequer," he said, and waited to see the effect of his words.

"Good Lord!" said my grandfather. "I'm a ruined man. I've been and given information against myself."

Then he laughed bitterly.

"At any rate," he said, "I ought to have the reward."

Mr. Symons slapped his thigh. "Exactly!" he said. "You take my meaning exactly. And why should you talk of ruin? I take it, Mr. Jeffrey, that you are clearly entitled to the reward offered to those who give information as to the whereabouts of smuggled goods. You find that people have been making unlawful use of your premises; you hold your peace until business brings you here at the week's end; then you come and acquaint me with the affair. Why should you talk of ruin?"

All this he said quite seriously, and talking rather more plainly than usual, as if he were teaching a lesson to a child. But my grandfather fell back in a chair and stared at him humbly; then he burst into a laugh, and the lawyer's face changed.

"That is all right, then," he said. "Come

into my parlour and we'll talk the matter out over a glass of something hot.

An hour later the riding-officers came. The chief of them was shown into the room, and stood stiff and dumb with amazement when he saw the company he was in.

"And what vexes me, Mr. Symons," my grandfather was saying, as he stirred up the sugar in his glass, "is that the villains may have been using my barn for years."

Then the riding-officer did not even try to tell his tale. My grandfather lost the spirits, and of course the reward never came his way. But to the end of his life he always had the greatest respect for Lawyer Symons.

# THE SPELL OF THE SEA

K

# THE SPELL OF THE SEA

WITH Cornishmen the love of country—or
of county—often goes so far as to lose the
name of virtue.    There is no place better
to live in, or to love in ; doubtless, also,
there is snug lying for the dead.    But—
since the fat of the land is his who will go
fetch it—he is no other than a fool that is
content to cling to a white-walled cottage
and bare bread in that "rocky land" of
people glad and proud to be "strangers"
to all but their kith and kin.

There is none in all that country but is
greatly tempted to this form of folly ; but,
upon the other hand, the sea lies round
about it—north and south, and in the
region of the sunset—continually calling,
calling.    And the call is one that no man
has been able to ignore.    So it is that to
whatever place you may go throughout the
world you will surely chance upon a little
band of Cornishmen, the most of whom
live very frugally, that presently they may

go home to take their ease where alone
contentment is possible. Meanwhile, the
half of their goods is at the command of
any stranger who can talk with the proper
affection of Tallywarn Street, in Tallywarn,
and truthfully aver that he has heard such
and such a local celebrity preach.

Even when they have made money and
gone home there is no end to their restless-
ness. A man is never so old but he may be
tempted by good wages and the opportunity
for change to go for a year or two to Ecua-
dor, or Mexico, or India; indeed, if there
be one found who has not yet travelled, you
may surely prophesy, seeing him stricken
in years, that he will shortly be doing so.
For these men have something of the sea
in their very blood, and sooner or later its
call is beyond resisting.

The miner's toil is of the sort that leaves
but little desire for active exercise; and
you would hardly look to him for rapt
appreciation of natural beauty. Yet, go
when you will to the cliffs beyond the
towns, you will find one or two of these
men wandering with no definite purpose,
alone, and manifestly happy.

One calls to mind a boy who went
long since from those parts to a school
in Somerset. Doubtless the country was

exceeding beautiful; but as the weeks
went by a desperate longing took possession of him; a holiday drew near, and he
inquired of all his comrades as to where
he would most wisely go in order to look
upon the sea. In the end he took train to
Minehead—and beheld, beyond a stretch
of dreadful slime, the muddy waters of
the Bristol channel, lazily breaking in
spiritless brown waves. It was on that
day he first came upon the green hair-
streak butterfly, and no doubt the capture
greatly rejoiced him. But the holiday re-
mained a disastrous disappointment, and
he was not ashamed to admit (to himself)
that he was become strangely homesick all
at once.

He is grown older now: he has so
much of the sea in memory that he can
never again be completely beggared of
felicity.

But a while ago he found great comfort,
during a long spell of night watching, in
the exercise of an unflagging fancy. When
the burden of watching grew most tiresome
he would close his eyes a moment, and lean
back in his chair; and in that very instant
he was carried away from the sick-room.
He was lying upon cool sands, and through
partly closed lids beheld the clear waves

breaking twenty yards away; he knew there were rounded pebbles within reach of his hand, yet was too happy to grope for one, and fling it lazily towards the sea. And in a moment he would open his eyes, refreshed, and take up again the task of watching.

He has also the common love of summer: of splendid sunshine, of blue skies, hazy with the heat that lies like a weightier lucent atmosphere along the southern cliffs. Already the bloom is all faded from the gorse, whereon the fleshy dodder shines against the sun like a tangle of clean copper wire. The chances are that he who goes afield finds himself absolute lord of league after league of honey-scented flowering heather; the seagulls float and fade silently overhead, the very butterflies are drowsy with the heat; only the larks have heart to sing, while bees are busy among the heather. In the same laziness one lets the sunlight do its work of restoration, while great waves rise in crystal, break, and die in murmuring foam on hot white beaches. One gathers no strength, it may be, to encounter the troubles that shall come; but (what is better) one can forget that such things have existed, or imagine them only the sombre background of his own blessed immunity.

Herein is great cause for gratitude; yet he is probably most true to his Cornish birth who finds the hot sunlight a thing unfamiliar and disconcerting — even as another might be vaguely displeased if the lady he loved should take to dressing her pretty tresses in a manner absolutely different from that she used when first he met with and, beholding, worshipped her.

There is much misguided talk of "Celtic melancholy," but it is the indisputable fact that the Cornishman loves best the seas that run high when the heather is faded, or has yet to open. There are clear skies and vast windy clouds; the colour of the sea is infinitely varied, from the deep blue of the distance to the softened green of the near waters, and every moment it changes; the thunder of the waves fills all the country side, and though a mile inland one still smells the brine upon the wind, and sees great clots of yellowish foam go by.

The Cornishman can answer to this mood of passionate activity; none can more heartily "pity the dead," that are beyond all restless stirrings of the spirit. But there is something prevents his enjoying, or putting himself in the posture to enjoy, the gross and drowsy pleasure men take when the heather blooms, and the hot air quivers along the cliffs.

But, after all, the spell of the sea comes with supreme force only upon such as have loitered long and frequently in some small harbour among the fisher-folk. One may be still a solitary, yet with a splendid sense of being comrade to all the world. One may be idle, but conscience troubles him no whit as he watches the endless activity of men and lads, and hearkens to the mingling of their voices with cries and laughter of half-naked children.

Under the green piles of an old and broken jetty the water laps most plea-santly: with a sound that inland folk may enjoy at a certain point in the churning of cream to butter; the very gulls, that, as you watched them from the cliffs, seemed the true children of those inhospitable regions, circle and swoop and cry above the harbour with a subtle differ-ence that gives the same absolute appro-priateness to their presence here.

He is most fortunate who has some such place to which he may resort as the last remedy against distresses of mind or body. Of a Monday forenoon he will watch the great boats poled out until they lie in a

# The Spell of the Sea

bunch before the harbour. The fishermen presently come down, each carrying the food of many days in a white linen bag; they gather on the "Ka-ay," and wait until the hired punts convey them to their boats. Each group has its own chief and hero, whose voice is loudest in discourse; the women have also come down, and there is no end to talk and laughter as the men go forth to their work. Until the last of the boats has tacked and tacked again before the harbour, and finally got clear of the land, there is no lack of occupation for the idler.

Afterwards, throughout the week, there are always boats returning, and hand-bells ringing upon the beach to announce the public sale of whatever fish they have taken. Even though there be no very obvious activity, it is good to linger in places where character of some sort has been caught, and fixed upon the faces of the people by the wind and salt spray; one develops a strange weariness of the folk who have lived the sheltered life, and wear dull masks instead of living faces.

At the week's end, when all the boats come in, one has no small share in the inevitable excitement: in the greeting of wives and sweethearts, the pride of donning holiday clothes and shiny boots, and faring forth to chat and chaff in the busy narrow streets, or to take part in a prayer-meeting at the Primitive Chapel. There are nights when the drift-boats fill the bay with tossing lights; there are whole weeks in autumn when all the world goes mad over the work of securing, landing, and curing the pilchards which the seiners, after many days of watching, have enclosed in their huge nets. And there is this gain beyond the mere delight of the eye: one loses quickly all sense of artificial distinctions, and comes to judge men with no prejudice save that which favours honesty, and good humour, and that cleanliness of the spirit that comes to men whose work is by the sea. It is realised that common humanity is a bond of union no accidental differences of class, of education, of experience, can destroy; and for this benignant sense of comradeship with all men one is most grateful to the sea that taught it.

And yet—How to forget its horrible secrets? Storm and wreck are the work of God's appointment, and, though they terrify, they can scarce affect with horror. It is the little things, the unsuspected hideousnesses, that abide and work within the mind.

# The Spell of the Sea

Listen, a moment, to another adventure of the boy already mentioned. Dawn set the thrushes singing one morning in a tiny orchard overlooked by the room wherein he slept; the boy awoke and listened; then, as the sense of a world already waking grew on him, he was resolved to waste no more of his time in sleep. He arose and dressed; very quietly he descended the scoured white stairs of the cottage, and in a moment he was faring gaily through the sleeping village. His spirits rose as he went: he felt himself proprietor of the great world, and for simple gladness of heart dashed hither and thither, when he had reached the sandy waste-lands, chasing the ridiculous rabbits.

At last the hush of the sea was more than a breathing whisper; he had come to where the sandhills slope down steeply to the beach.

"Once, in a land beside the Western sea,
When morning brake and o'er the level sands
Grey mists went seaward with the ebbing tide. . . ."

Somehow his gaiety went from him as he looked on the cold sands, the grey, abject sea. But he quickly recovered his spirits when he had descended to the beach, and set forth upon an exploration of the tide-mark. He discovered a score of useless treasures, and began to have ideas upon the wisdom of early rising; when he looked ahead, and espied a huge and shapeless mass of seaweed. A certain sense of solitariness came over him as he drew near, but he had scarce become conscious of it when he stood above the shapeless pile, investigating it curiously with outstretched foot. Then, suddenly, the weeds slid and parted, and he beheld a white hand, hideously swollen, and still clutching as it had clutched vainly in the moment of death.

He knew that this tame sea he had been despising had left a dead man upon the shore as it retreated, and immediately he turned and fled. The rustle of the grey sand-grasses thrilled him with a nameless horror; he almost shrieked aloud when a rabbit started suddenly from beneath his feet; the quiet village mocked him with its atmosphere of death : and until the people arose and went cheerfully about the day's toil he was still doomed to behold that swollen, clutching hand.

And yet . . . . It was years afterwards he found himself homesick for the sea.

# THE BIBLE READER

" But there!" said Sam'l, as he reached the end of his story. "There's a bra' many Christians, as they do call themselves, that do read the Bible in no better fashion than old John Sampson. . . . . G'wan Jess!"

He shook up the reins and awaited the question he knew would not be long delayed.

"Who was old John Sampson?" I asked.

"Another of the many people that I knew before you came into these parts," was the answer. "Wheal Dream had not been stopped in those days, and John Sampson came from over to Tallywarn to work there, and took lodgings with mother, for she was a widow and hard pushed to find food and home for a family of young children."

"And he did not read his Bible very wisely?" I persisted.

Sam'l chuckled. "He didn' read it all

first going away," he answered. "Mother was a woman of some conscience: she used to wonder whether it wadn' laid upon her to turn him to doors and starve, rather than have such a man under a Christian roof. I believe he was sober enough and no great swearer. Indeed, so far as I can remember him, he was one that hardly ever talked about anything. But he never went to chapel, nor even to church, all the time he was lodging wi' mother. He used to spend Sundays out upon the moors in good weather, and when it rained he would sit smoking in a little shed where the donkey-cart was kept. If he was by when mother prayed before sending us off to bed he would go outside and sit on the garden wall with his pipe in his mouth. I've known her pull down the window and pray almost in a shout, on the chance that some word in season might strike him like a javelin and bring him to a proper state of mind.

"He stopped in Pentreath for some years, and 'twas always the same with him. Then one day he came into the kitchen with a very strange look upon his face. 'Beggin' your pardon, Mis' Gurney,' he said, 'but could 'ee give me the loan of a Bible?'

# The Bible Reader

"I can see mother's face now, for I was growing a big boy by this time. 'A Bible?' she said. 'Thee's want a Bible?'

"'Iss,' he said, 'if there's one handy.'

"'Praise be for that!' she said. 'I'll give 'ee a Bible.'

"Well, she gave him a Bible, and after that she watched him pretty closely. And, 'Ah,' she said one day, 'the influence of a Christian family is a thing that must tell.' For old John Sampson stuck to that Bible like a limpet to a rock, and was all the time reading it. Mother noticed that he began at the beginning and read straight through, genealogies and all; and that pleased her, for she was always thorough herself.

"This went on for some little time. There was a bra' deal of talk about it in Pentreath, and to begin with very few would believe the story mother told. However old Mis' Skewes dropped in one evening—all by chance, as she made out—and sure enough John Sampson was sitting in the doorway, reading away for dear life. So she went forth and told the news all over Pentreath, and there was no end to talk and wonder.

"Mother was pleased enough to have

matters as they were for a time. However, after a bit, she thought 'twas a pity the old man shouldn' go further, having begun so well. So one Sunday morning, when he took up the Bible and was going out to sit on the little seat that stood against the front of the house, she spoke.

" 'Wouldn' 'ee like to come to chapel, John?' she said.

" He looked back with a curious bit of a smile on his face. 'No,' he said, 'I'd rather stop here and read the Bible.'

" 'Well,' said mother, 'I suppose you do know what's best for 'ee.'

"Very soon John Sampson went into town one Saturday by Jimmy Hayle's van, and brought back a fat red book, that turned out to be a dictionary. After that he always had the two books by him at the same time. He would stop in the midst of his Bible-reading and turn over the leaves of his dictionary like a man hunting for something. But he never seemed to find it—whatever it might be. And presently he finished the last chapter of *Revelation*, and shut up the book with the air of a man come to the end of a long job and not too well pleased with what he'd done. He laid it down upon the table.

" 'I suppose you haven' got another

Bible in the house?' he said. 'I should like to get the loan of it if you have.'

"'Why man,' said mother, 'isn't your own Bible, that I gave 'ee, good enough for 'ee? What difference is there between one Bible and another?'

"'If you've got another,' he said, 'I should like to get the loan of it.'

"Well, mother was only too glad to have the old man read the Bible at all. She humoured him and fetched out the great, big Family Bible. And he began again at *Genesis* and went right on to *Revelation*. He still kept the dictionary by him as he read, and would still turn away from his reading about once in ten minutes to hunt in that dictionary for something he never seemed to find. More than once mother hinted about his going to chapel, but his answer was always the same. 'No,' he would say, 'I'd rather stop at home and read the Bible.'

"When he came to the end of the Family Bible a strange story began to be told about him. For he went forth and borrowed another Bible and commenced again at *Genesis*. At the end of a year he had come to *Revelation* again, and then he went and borrowed another Bible. 'Twould be a bold thing to say a man was touched in the head and gone totelish because he was all the time reading the Scriptures. But what puzzled every one was that John Sampson should never be willing to read the same copy of the Book more than once.

"At last, after much talk upon the subject, every one was convinced that he really was a little bit dotty; for a man came into Pentreath selling cheap Bibles, and John bought three copies, varying in size like three children o' one family. He put two in his drawer, and went through the other in the usual way, turning aside continually to hunt in the dictionary for something that he never seemed to find.

"I was a young man by this time, and working in the same pare with him at Wheal Dream. 'Twas common practice for some of the younger men to laugh at him about his Bible-reading, but they couldn' do so very openly, for the elder men wouldn' hear of it.

"'Perhaps he is mazed,' said one of them. 'But 'twould be a good thing for Pentreath if the whole of you was touched with the same madness.'

"Now, can 'ee guess what he read the Bible for? No need to answer, for you wouldn' be right if you guessed till Dooms-day. Nor did any one in Pentreath ever dream of what had worked the change until John Sampson died suddenly, when he was about half-way through the third of his Bibles. Of course they searched his drawers and so on. And at last they found an old pocket-book. In it was a piece cut out of the 'All Sorts' column of the *Argus*:

"'Any one who discovers a printer's mistake in a copy of the Bible is entitled to receive a reward of one guinea.'

"Mother was very much surprised to find how much the old man's savings amounted to: 'twas plain he must have been a miser. And, knowing that, she couldn' misunderstand the meaning of that bit of newspaper. John had read the Scriptures daily for years past in the hope of finding a mistake in the spelling of it, and earning a guinea. Whether he would have got it, I can't say; for he certainly never found a mistake. And yet I could never get mother to own up that all that reading of the Scriptures wouldn' stand to his credit for so much as a halfpenny, being undertaken in a wrong spirit."

Sam'l ceased, and flourished an ineffectual-looking whip. " Now, make haste Jess," he said ; " 'tis late, and I got to go to prayer-meeting to-night."

But Jess jogged onward at the old sober pace, that nothing could alter, and Pentreath was still miles away.

# MARGUERITE IN LONDON

## I

FOR a long time after he entered into possession the man looked upon his chambers merely as a place to sleep and to do work in : his life and leisure were spent outside. He had been living in suburban lodgings, with a wall-paper to which no sensitive person could have dreamed of introducing an object of beauty. Moreover, he was as poor as one needs to be.

Yet he had in him the desire of possessing, and the love of beautiful things, and so there came a time when he was owner of many treasures. He had learned that "bread is the food of the body, but narcissus is the food of the soul": that a good dinner is no more than a bad one when it has been eaten a few hours, while even a moderately good Delft pot, or a colour-print after so small a master as Yeizan, is in its degree a joy for ever.

# Marguerite in London

Then Marguerite came into his life. The man soon thought of eternity as a thing infinitely less than time, for he had known Marguerite for ever (as it now seemed), yet he could remember the date of his entering the chambers. For a little space (if I am rightly informed) they spent their precious hours in restaurants and theatres. They always parted with a sense of having wasted time: for what author ever wrote anything of such importance as the trifles they had not found time to discuss? They met only once in a month, or in three, and so they had much to say, for each had the faculty of observation, and each the gift of enjoying little things keenly.

Once they had been apart for longer than usual, and it seemed they must have great matters to communicate. Yet the thing he chiefly desired to tell her was that he had been to a studio in Fitzroy Square one dismal October day, and come depressed out of that squalid region into Tottenham Court Road—where cheapness is the only quality boasted of, and no one ever dreams of saying that his wares are good. Then he had seen a girl with beautiful fair hair, and a blouse of poppy-red silk; and, behold, his depression had vanished, and he had gone happy to his work, and enshrined the

blouse in verse before the day was out. In
the interval that had elapsed since their last
meeting he had had his small successes, but
this was the episode he most desired to
resurrect, and her pride meant less to him
than her enjoyment of that vanished glint
of scarlet.

So things moved naturally. Then he
looked at her one day while they waited for
their coffee. Her dress was like a daffodil,
all gold and white, and he paused in the
act of speech to admire it once again. " I
couldn't make up my mind about a theatre.
Have you any choice ? "

" None at all," she said.

He looked at his watch, and then glanced
around the little crowded restaurant. " We
must decide quickly if we are to go. Why
do the theatres begin so early ? The best
of our dinner would be to come if we had
not to hurry."

An interval ensued, while the friendliest
waiter in London filled their cups. " Is
there anything you want to see ? " asked
the man.

" Nothing," she answered.

" Then we'll play at being in Paris.
There is one place where you may do
that."

All night a band played, and they supped

coffees and *menthe et l'eau*, and such-like things, talking vigorously. But at the end the man was again conscious of a night whose opportunities had somehow been neglected. And so when another blessed evening brought them together, there was a repetition of the scene.

"Do you know that you have never seen the chambers?" said he.

"I thought you had forgotten," said she.

"You will come?"

"Do you suppose I have not wanted to come? Do you realise how you have boasted?"

It need only be told of that particular night that they discovered another point of agreement, in that both loved the soft light of candles beyond all other modes of illumination. The point is a small one, but it was a part of their experience that a coincidence of taste in trifles weighs more heavily in the balance than the biggest of differences. Afterwards the man lost count of the number of her visits, and could only remember of such and such an event that it happened "once, when you came." But Marguerite had each separate visit by heart, and sometimes dismayed him by her minute remembrance of the individual days in an eternity.

# Marguerite in London

Their conversation was always of this kind. They forgot personalities when they had reached their harbour of refuge, and talked only of trifles that, having pleased one or the other, interested both.

The man was poor, or his London chambers might soon have been changed for a suburban villa. But he had the collector's passion, and he could not pretend that he did not love the things he had gathered around him. He had a way of slipping his mistaken purchase out of sight, and you will understand how it was that he had an accident with a blue and white bowl, incautiously bought by gas-light, soon after he had seen it by the disenchanting rays of the sun, and observed the inkiness of colour. But the bulk of his possessions were to him like a well-beloved family; and there was always a Benjamin—the latest acquisition.

Marguerite professed to be mighty scornful of them all, and she was also severe upon his extravagance. There were times when she professed to believe him an uncanny creature, capable of affection only for the things that are bought at a price in out-of-the-way second-hand shops. Indeed, she was never told how he grew to regard his chambers as a place where things that would please her had to be collected; or how he came to feel that something unseen before must await her at each visit. He knew that she loved all that was beautiful, and her protestations of indifference left him unmoved.

Once, indeed—and perhaps on many occasions—he laid a little trap for her. She had declared full often that the art of Japan was hateful to her, knowing that it fascinated him. He was serenely confident in her good taste, and so on this occasion the only new acquisition was a colour-print after Harunobu, a lovely harmony in delicate greens. It was framed, but he did not hang it, and his walls were so fully occupied that the question of finding it a place was one of obvious difficulty. It leant against his bookcase, the face of it hidden, when they got to the rooms.

She took her wonted seat. Never did she appear to scrutinise the contents of his room, yet presently, with a distinct note of disappointment, she said, "Why, there is nothing new!"

"Hard up!" he answered. "But there's a print."

"Where is it" she asked.

"I didn't know you cared for that sort of thing; here it is."

She held the frame at arm's length for

awhile, regarding the picture. " You can't
see it by this light," he said presently.
" Those lovely greens want daylight."

Marguerite was positively enthusiastic.
" It is the best you've got," she said.

" Yes," he said ; " it cost about as much
as all the others put together. The bother
is that I cannot think of a place for it.
It will kill all the others."

" Where did you propose to put it ? "

He showed her, revealing at the same
time his consciousness of the unsuitability
of the place. " No," she said, " That
won't do."

Is it necessary to continue ? The man's
housekeeper had one saving merit : she
did not attempt to combat the dust that
continually invaded his rooms. In a minute
or two Marguerite had begun to be openly
interested. With a few deft touches she
made some magic change in her apparel,
so that dust need not be feared. Then
the two were deep in the grave business of finding a place for the Harunobu. All sorts of changes were made,
until the atmosphere was thick with dust.
But at last they believed that they were
satisfied, and then it was time to descend
and take a cab.

But Marguerite was henceforth unable

to pretend that the man's possessions were not dear to her. For on the next occasion of her coming to town she betrayed herself when they had been scarce ten minutes together." "Have you moved the Harunobu?" she asked. "I've come to the conclusion that we didn't choose the right place, after all."

"I am sure of it," he said. "We will have another sitting to-night."

THE day should have been Pleasure's own,
for Marguerite was in London, and the im-
patient Spring had come early that it might
meet her there. Along the Strand there
were flowers everywhere: huge baskets of
sweet violets at street corners, and daffodils
going to the suburbs on the top of every
'bus. The sky had a brilliance that was
almost disconcerting; the air was a caress.
It seemed that all women had donned
their brightest in the day's honour, and all
seemed fair.

Moreover, as it happened, the man had
no need to work that day, when to do anything but enjoy the act of living would
have appeared a profanation. But he came
out into the air with feelings not wholly in
tune with Nature. It was good to think
that he would drive with Marguerite
through many a mile of the loveliest streets
there are. But it would be a pleasure end-
ing in pain: he was to drive with her to

the station, whence she would take train to the country. He might not follow her; he had but newly made a discovery—to wit, that human eyes can be beautiful—and he was afraid lest, left alone, he might relapse into his old state, and forget this wonderful new knowledge.

Marguerite met him with a face that reflected his mood—which the sight of her intensified. They talked awhile, for the drive they had in prospect was well enough, but neither of them was eager to start. They spoke of the dinner of the night before, of the beauty of the day, of a buckle of old silver he had picked up in the course of his wanderings, and now brought as his parting gift. Then they were told that they would need to be going. There were farewells to be said before they were together in the hansom.

The streets were wonderful, and it seemed to them that the shops held no other merchandise than flowers, unless it were blue china and wonderful oak chests, and candlesticks of exquisite design in brass and Sheffield plate. All the beautiful children in London were abroad that morning, and Marguerite had a smile for all, had they but noted it as she passed. The two should have been depressed, for every moment brought them nearer to the parting that was so hateful. But the blessed morning triumphed, and they could only remember that they were together, and that to be alive was good.

Presently Marguerite looked at him under the wide brim of her amazing hat. " I don't believe that you are half so sorry as you ought to be."

He laughed. " I'll have time enough for sorrow presently. What a day it is ! "

A moment later he spoke in a changed voice. " A minute more and we are at the station. Why do you choose a train so early ? "

" You forget our country slowness," she said. " This is the only good one. If I chose another I should be four hours in the train."

" But there are others ? " he continued. " Then we will cheat the Fates, and have the happiness they would have denied us. Give me two more hours, and you shall laugh at an eternity of travel. Make me happy, and I will promise you shall be the same. Think of it : in all the years before us there may never be a morning like this. You will wait ? "

Again that look of hers ! His late discovery came home to him again like a new thing. "I shall be expected!" she said.

"Dear lady, generations of electricians have slaved that you and I may have these two hours that were not meant for us. You will wait?"

"It is as you like," she answered, glad to be compelled. So they reached the station, and descended quickly, eager to get the goodness out of every moment in their two hours.

"How is it," asked Marguerite, innocently, "that cabmen and railway porters always thank you so effusively? They are gruff enough with some people of my acquaintance."

"And with me when I haven't you! But I could scatter gold to-day. Have I told you of my rule? After these partings I travel back on a 'bus. It would seem wrong, somehow, if I were to go comfortably."

"What shall we do?" asked Marguerite, with a little movement of pleasure.

"Why," he said, "there is the shop where I bought the blue plates to be seen, and another where they have the most splendid things from time to time. You will not mind that the street is ugly, and the shop a lumber-room."

The change in the weather had influenced

even this dull, small street. The shops where the man was wont to come in quest of treasure had half their stock displayed upon the pavement. At the door of one a haggard woman was standing, and she watched the wanderers with interest when they fell into a dispute as to whether a certain lantern of brass was a treasure demanding to be acquired. Marguerite was good to look at. The woman, recognising the man, indulged in reflections, and smiled as she caught his companion's eye. Marguerite blushed like a rose.

"Is there no other place to see?" she asked; but she had smiled back at the woman before she turned away, blushing again as she realised how she had been betrayed.

It was soon after that they returned to wider thoroughfares, and sought a place to lunch at. A great hotel hard by the station was the only place that was possible, but it seemed a palace of delight. They sat at a little table, and a flood of light came through tall windows. What they ate I do not remember, but the waiter was a miracle of sympathy, and the wine they drank was but an inexpensive excuse for remembering certain verses:

# Marguerite in London

"Fill a glass with golden wine,
And the while your lips are wet,
Set their perfume unto mine,
And forget
Every kiss we take and give
Leaves us less of life to live."

The man did more than remember: he dared to quote. And Marguerite laughed at him across the flowers, with a little look around the room—where others were lunching—and the smallest possible shrug of regret. When it came to the coffee she burned his cognac, disregarding his protests at the waste of good spirit in a light that made the pretty flame invisible, leaving only the fizzling sugar to be watched.

At last, "Is it time to go?" she asked.

He paid his bill, and soon they were at the station. The guard marked them as his legitimate prey at once, and soon he had her locked up in an empty carriage, the prettiest of captives.

"Do you begin to be sorry?" she asked.

"I'll be sorry to-morrow," he said. "I have had my happiness to-day. . . . . If only I could always have you locked up —my captive—as you are now!"

"Do you think I am so free, then?" asked she.

# Marguerite in London

The train began to move. He touched her hand, and they said good-bye. Then she was gone, and he turned away to go back into an empty London. But the rule of which he had spoken had, like others, its exceptions. He hailed the nearest hansom and drove to his chambers swiftly and in comfort, blessing the day which had given him these two hours, and forgetting that Marguerite had before her four of irksome travel.

Later he wrote some verses :

"I will not move my hand to where
   I dream you sit with silken hair
      That waits for my caress : mine eyes
   Are hungry for the sight of you ;
   Yet are they closed, for still 'tis true
      Only the man who dreams is wise.

"Of wisdom I have scanty store,
   Nor dare take oath to err no more,
      But, O, my heart, I still shall hold
   To this my dream that comforts me :
   Where'er you wander, you will be
      Here where you came to me of old."

When they were done he began to realise that she had gone.

# THE SMELL OF THE GOOD
## EARTH

# THE SMELL OF THE GOOD EARTH

FROM the earth we came, and thither shall we return; but this certainty of death is the assurance of immortality. For the good earth renovates, and a man must needs "rise glorious" who has lain quiet a long time while the smell of it worked its will upon him. The story of Antæus is the truest ever man made: for from the earth alone, and from the great sea that is a part of it, does a man get strength.

There come to all of us seasons when existence (which should be compounded of innumerable small pleasures, resulting from the discharge of life's necessary duties) becomes altogether intolerable. Something is wrong with eye and brain: music is but a jarring noise, and there is no delight in any array of colour. The pen lies idle, or to use it is a wretched subjugation of instinct; you cannot think; that you should be conscious is a dreadful imposition; for

# The Smell of the Good Earth

the miserable days are endless, and the
nights bring neither sleep nor rest.

" When the sea calls, that lieth leagues away,
    Athwart the flaring city and the din,
This little room is Hell till dawn of day,
    And I a sinner damned for sordid sin.

" Better the long day and the dripping rain,
    The hateful cries of hawkers in the street,
Small, hateful tasks to do and do again :
    These let me dream my dream that rest is sweet."


Now, when it is come to this pitch, a man
must seek his own cure, and I fancy there
is but one medicine possible to each : one
way in which he can get back to the good
earth which restores him.   There are some
whose choice it is to go forth into the fields,
stopping much to talk with simple folk
whose daily work lies there ; at last a breath
of Spring comes (though it be dry summer)
into the air, and the goodness steals back
into their life.   Such men are for ever
looking before and after : they will not let
themselves believe that the past Spring is
altogether gone by until they have received
a sure token of the Spring that is to
come.

Another would find his health given back
most speedily if he should be permitted
to listen awhile to "streaming London's

# The Smell of the Good Earth

central roar "—to watch the great crowds that are not so much collections of individuals as masses of life in the concrete.

Another would go, if it were permitted him, to a small fishing-town at the foot of the Western hills. He would talk with the fisher-folk, and watch the numerous activities it is his chief desire to understand. At sunset he would still be idling on the deserted quay, watching the thicket of the masts standing out above the glory that crowned the hills, with yellow lights from the hillside caught among the spars. Later, it may be, you would find him in some small tavern where the fishermen congregate. But soon the little town would be quiet, and the man walking by the road which runs betwixt dark pinewoods, the sea so far below (though visible with its tossing lights) that its murmur seemed no more than the breathing of a world asleep. For to each man there is but one method of returning to the earth whence he draws strength.

Sometimes it would be best of all to lie (dead, indeed, but dimly conscious of the quiet) upon a bed of white sand, deep in some clear sea. For the voice of the sea, that knows no rest, speaks eloquently to the hearts of men, making it hardly possible they should remember their own small troubles that will end so quickly.

> " All the refuse of the city
>     Ever drifting to the sea ;
>     Foulness of the river merging
>     In the sea's cold purity.
>
> " Is life's current fouled, encumbered
>     With God's failures?  There doth lie
>     A vast sea beyond the river,
>     And the saddest soul must die."

But chiefly you desire, if ever the world is too much with you, to get back to a little wood, where you wandered in search of some indefinite and unattainable good while you were yet a child.  The noise of the wind among the leaves is with you, and there were always doves crooning somewhere in the inner recesses of the place.

But best of all is the earth below.  You might dig deep and still find nothing but the fallen leaves of many springtimes, and the good black earth into which they pass at last.  If one could lie here, buried a few feet underground, and still dimly conscious, as perhaps the trees and stones are conscious!  The black earth would lie lightly, and its scent in your nostrils would be like knowing the hand of the good God upon you.

# The Smell of the Good Earth

Body and spirit would be young again, and the son of Mother Earth draw nourishment, like a human child, from her generous breast. If it it were written he should presently awake, he would in truth rise glorious ; and if the sleep were lasting, who but must envy him still?

For who is more happy than the child that sleeps?

# NEW YEAR'S EVE

N

I HARDLY know for how long I had sat gazing into the fire when I first became aware of the stranger: a very pleasant gentleman who stood patiently waiting until I should discover him. "I break upon your meditations?" he said. "I trust I have not erred in my choice of time and place?"

"Upon my soul, sir," I answered, "I did meditate—upon nothing. You have in nowise erred. Sit you down, and welcome: for I discern in you a gentleman made for companionship, and perceive that I have been over long a solitary. Come, be seated, I entreat you."

He laughed pleasantly, and settled, like an old friend who demands but the smallest show of welcome, in the great chair beside my own. "And so you keep your watchnight alone?" he said.

"Why, sir," I answered, "I would hesitate to judge the race upon the evidence

of my personal choice ; yet surely there is
no man would desire to keep his watchnight otherwise?   But, to be candid, I had
no thought of the occasion ; I merely
drowsed by the fireside, reflecting that the
world was somewhat unamusing."

"You slept, in fine, as a plenty of good
people are sleeping still in the pews of your
chapels.   Yet every moment while you
slept the end of the year drew nigh, and
the year's record approached its end.   Had
you no desire to snatch a victory at the last
moment: to discover some small nobility,
were it only of thought, wherewith to gild
the meanness of that chronicle?   For you
have failed, I take it, with the common ruck
of men: in effort as in achievement?"

"I have told you," I said, "I have told
you I had no thought of the season ; and I
perceived no unwonted alacrity in the flight
of time.   Least of all had I the desire to
tamper with the record of my failures.
Why, sir, it is my constant effort to forget
that such a chronicle exists within this
brain of mine.   I have seen each page
while it was in the writing ; I know that
the prophecy of my future lies therein ;
but I can still refrain from turning back
to disquiet myself with old unalterable
writings."

# New Year's Eve

"Ay," said my friend and visitor; "what is written remains, indelible. A man may brood upon his record, but his past is for ever what it was. You are wise in your refusal to look back. But what of resolves for the future: surely you are permitted a certain control over destiny? You may resolve to have, and will have if you resolve, a record for the future that shall not be altogether ignoble: to make the new leaf in your book of life one that some day may tempt you to turn back and read. It is the eve of the New Year: have you no New Year's resolve?"

"Resolve?" I cried. "I protest I am weary of resolves; I am most weary of this talk of New Year's pledges. You may dissever the hand's act from the brain's, but never year from year in a man's life, nor day from day. If I were made sole master of this present I might achieve some small thing that would please you: at the very least, I promise you, my thoughts should have the nobility you advise. But past and future invade my territory of the present, and I am tenant only by their good-will."

The stranger moved uneasily in his seat, then was still again and smoothed the beard upon his chin. "You hold yourself the bound slave of destiny?" he said.

"Why, sir," I said, "I have the power to withdraw from your pleasing company, quitting this tabernacle of the flesh that I ennoble. But it is denied me to know whether I shall then be mere clay, or shall look curiously out of another sphere (as I have looked on ant-hills by the roadway) upon the life I have abandoned. And though my personal identity be the veriest figment, I cling to it and will not explore the dark until I must. Beyond this privilege of risking everything—of rushing on a disastrous enlightenment—I am surely master of nothing at all? For all our talk of past and present, there is no past in the history of our race. God knows myself am by no means undesirous of well-doing: it were the natural choice of a man to cut a handsome figure before the world. But my present is but the child of the dead ages, the scapegoat of the generations gone by. I am come to years of wisdom: for comfort's sake I would fain walk discreetly. But I have no sooner willed it than I am mastered by some dead ancestor: a man or woman long since forgotten in the grave; oftener by the fool, my old self of years past. A century since a man fell into evil ways and went drunken to his death; his children suffered, and many that never heard his name; and now myself must needs tremble like a Methody at the smell of wine, and shun all natural pleasure. There was a foolish nurse that told her idiot stories to a child scarce out of the cradle; I am the weaker for his dreadful nights. Most of all it is that old self baulks my efforts to do well. I am a person of no extraordinary ambitions: at most I hunger after no greater righteousness than the general voice would impose upon me. I would speak the truth, but must needs lie lest the dead fool go dishonoured in his grave for his untruthfulness; I would fain bear with my adversary, but his unchastened passions are beyond my control. I am the latest flower of all the ages; but remember, I pray you, who had the planting of this tree by poisonous waters, and what infinite evil chances have marred the growth of that from which I am sprung. I protest I am guiltless of immodesty; yet do I tell you I am as good as I could be."

I had talked vehemently, growing angry with the gods that made me, plaguing me with this delusion that I, a simple part in the life of the world, was a man permitted to regard himself apart from his environment, a living soul responsible to God. I had not observed the bearing of my visitor; but now I beheld him eagerly bending towards me, as if he were fain to speak.

"Tell me," I said. "You would remark that the fool I have been scorning is scarce yet wholly dead in me?"

"The past, indeed, invades your present," he said. "I have heard little of the intruding future. Yet for the future's sake I dare still exhort you to fresh resolves of well-doing. Flower is seed, remember; you who are mastered by the past create the past of others, and shall have that mastery dead which has been denied you living. It would comfort you to be assured of a real individuality? Let it suffice for your assurance that you will fix the destiny of unnumbered men and women. Why, sir, it may well be that for this night that you have spent in idle clamour against the gods a man unborn will pay the penalty in a will incapable of resolve, a spirit unable to stand firm in good or evil. But though the nearest past be beyond redemption you have still the shaping of the present. Even now the clock is upon the hour of midnight, and a year is gone; for the future's sake I pray you condescend to vulgar repentance

# New Year's Eve

and be to no man hereafter a part of his creator's malice."

He ceased, and immediately I was aware of footsteps in the streets. The good people were returning from their chapel, and I stood and watched them as they passed in the moonlight : eager for their beds, yet finding time for kindly New Year greetings.

Last of all came two that were younger. They passed close beneath my window, so that this speech came to me clearly on the frosty air : "Of course it is the longest way. Why, I shall always take the longest way to a parting from you!" I watched them vanish into the deep blue shadow.

" For the sake of the future!" I said, as I turned to resume the conversation.

I was vastly surprised. He had come so quietly, he was now as swiftly gone! I guessed at once that what I have told you could have been no more than a dream.

Printed by BALLANTYNE, HANSON & Co.
London & Edinburgh